Bennu Bright

COMPASS
TO MY
HEART

An MM Compass-Born Fated Mate
Fantasy Romance

Also by Bennu Bright

Romantic Fantasy

The Demon Lord of California: The Demon and the Phoenix, book 1

Fantasy Romance

Compass To My Heart: Compass-Born Trilogy, book 1

Short Stories

A Phoenix Halloween Fantasy Ball (Romance)

Gritty Epic Fantasy Rising from the Ashes by 2027 (formerly published under Jeanne Marcella)

Through Rain and Missing Mantaurs
The Phoenix Embryo

First edition October 31, 2023
Second edition November 2023
Second edition print November 2025

Print ISBN: 979-8-9998831-3-1
Ebook ISBN: 979-8-9998831-2-4

https://www.bennubright.com

Ebook design and print design by Bennu Bright

Cover art, and Lune & Narsus portraits by Lara Yokoshima

Phoenix forge illustrations by APHOTICMOTH

Content Placard

COMPASS TO MY HEART is a male/male fantasy romance novel.

- Possibly steamy or spicy/sexually suggestive/risqué scenes.

- Blunt language of and handling of body parts.

- Possibly the presence of graphic swear words.

- (Vampires) death, dying, resurrection, undead. Thirst for blood, desire to bite.

- Fire, burning, burning alive.

- Fear of water, drowning. PTSD/passing recollections of a shark attack.

- PTSD/death of a loved one. A character experiencing their own multiple deaths.

- Brief, passing reference to drinking/alcoholism.

Synopsis

Compass To My Heart is a MM fantasy romance about marriage by proxy, one bed, a poisoned kiss, and fated mate shifters finding each other through compasses created by ancient magic.

Lune doesn't know much about his mystical birthright as a Compass-born, yet its promise of a life-mate cushions the long days and lonely nights. So he patiently waits, eager for when the compass will point him in the direction he must go.

Touch-starved Narsus is a Verdigris—a highly toxic phoenix with poisonous feathers. To be Compass-born, as well as undead, are additional torturous and heartbreaking burdens. So he hides away in heavy cloaks and a beaked mask to protect those around him.

When the compass calls, Narsus further ostracizes himself by sending a proxy to the marriage ceremony, for he no longer believes in love. Or destiny.

Hurt and embarrassed, Lune is determined to crack Narsus's emotional armor. To show his Intended there's always hope. But with the compasses counting down, can Lune convince Narsus to take a chance on love?

Prologue

HE WAS A TINY bubble, bobbing in the choppy ocean. Aimlessly floating along the currents. Scared. So alone. Not understanding or knowing how he came to be here.

He wasn't sure how he knew, but in his mind's eye, he witnessed the infinite world around him rocking and tilting, moving this way, then that. His universe was a blue-green blur except for the larger, ominous shapes sometimes looming near. Sometimes they lunged, as if they wanted to devour him, but the current carried him away—just in time. Sometimes his little universe went dark, as if he had been devoured, but spit back out again. His escalation of fear never lasted long, for it was kept at bay by the strange, glowing, metallic seed he'd wrapped himself around.

This seed was something he'd always had. It was a part of him. It was the only thing that soothed him. Sustained him. It was so cozily warm and safe. Protecting him. Guiding him to where he needed to be, although he didn't yet understand where that was.

Then he was here, swirling around in a place where the colors were brighter, crisper. Water continuously shoved him up against some slimy rocks and the sun sparkled above. But the jostling soon took its toll. Making tiny cracks in his round, gelatinous, self-contained bubble. The silvery seed he clung to mended these cracks, but with each new fissure, the repairs lessened. He was getting tired, and very sleepy, despite the sun suddenly growing warmer, coming closer.

His drowsiness faded away when a shadow fell over him. Within, there was a pale face, distorted by the ripples of the water. Gentle energy flooded the life back into him, feeding him, lulling him, protecting him.

The face was replaced by the approach of cupped hands. His universe shook as he was scooped up. The face came closer.

He wasn't sure how he knew, but this being was Calico.

"Affirmative, my little ocean-peep," Calico greeted warmly. "We communicate jointly through telepathy, and your ability to echo locate. Hello, little one. So you are the source of this ancient magic drawing me."

The sound of that cheerful, guttural voice should have frightened him. But it didn't.

"Your siren's song brings notes of beauty, but lucky for myself, you are still too young to mesmerize. It appears you have had a very rough journey." Calico looked out across the ocean, as if scanning.

Nestled within his tiny bubble, he didn't know how, but he sensed the wave of Calico's telepathy curl about their little cove, then beyond. Searching. For something. Or someone. There was only silence from the beyond.

"You poor, precious water bean," Calico told him. "Not even your song found them. Yes, you are so very alone. But no longer—"

Calico cut himself off. "Oh, my!"

There was a longer pause, where he was raised up to Calico's eye level. He lost himself in the welcoming, colorful swirls of Calico's cheerful, brilliant blues.

"You are a Compass-born, little one. I should have known by the resonance of your magical call! Oh, your Compass-seed is quite strong indeed."

So that's what he held onto for dear life. His Compass-seed had protected him all this time.

"I shall safeguard you for transport." Calico gently poured him into a small glass tube. "I think I shall call you Lune. Oh! I beg your pardon; this has been most rude of me. I have not properly introduced myself. My name is Calico, of the Breese phoenix forge. I am a god who is the physical embodiment of space-time, but I much prefer spending my days in the kitchen. Come, my dear siren fry-child, let us return home. I have a cozy beach house with a gentle tidepool which I think you will enjoy. You shall finish germinating where the current is not so harsh, and where I can guard you against the hungry."

Lune. He liked that name very much. So he lessened his desperate terror-grip on the little Compass-seed that strained to protect him. He was no longer alone. He was finally safe. With a family found.

Chapter 1

Lune surfaced, blinking waterdrops from his eyelashes. He took his compass out of his mouth and hooked it back onto his belt. He'd learned how to hold onto it the hard way.

The last time he'd done hull inspections on the Jade Raptor, his precious compass had slipped loose from his belt. It'd taken him two hours of sifting through sand and silt at the bottom of the harbor to find it.

That had been the most frantic, heart-pounding two hours of his life. Even more terrifying and traumatic than the time he'd been attacked by a shark. So much so that he now went to the blacksmith every six months to have the rivets and hooks on his belt inspected for durability.

Lune knew his compass was secure at his hip, because of his precautions, and it was how he usually wore the directional instrument. But today he felt extra anxious about it.

His compass was no ordinary bit of equipment. It was pure magic sculpted into a compass. Its purpose was to locate, and connect with his fated mate when the time was right. Someone he could spend his life with. So he wouldn't have to be alone. If that's what he really wanted.

Compass-marriages were strange and mysterious customs. They were few and very far between. They were revered and awed. Even he wasn't exactly sure what it all meant. All he knew was that somewhere in the world, his Intended was in possession of a matching compass.

Here in the harbor, the little waves lapping at his neck were as cool and refreshing as it was beyond the reefs. It took a second to re-tie his wavy blond hair so the sopping wet strands wouldn't get caught in his gills.

The water's purity was in thanks to the harbormaster and her affinity with said element. Along with that, a little bit of purchased magic to help keep the waterways clean was like a guard dog who never slept.

Lune lingered with his inspections, bobbing around the hull of his beloved boat. Scrutinizing and testing every inch of the barnacle-scraped wood. They were damn lucky this time. There were just a couple of cosmetic scuffs below the waterline.

Being up the entire night, pacing during the worst storm of the season, had stressed him out. His fifty-foot passenger boat had been knocked around. She'd slipped her moorings, and been swept out. Lune thanked the gods his assigned space was a straight shot out into the wilds, else he could've been responsible for damage to other craft. But his Jade Raptor was back now, and safely in the arms of her doting parents.

Lune heaved a sigh of relief, and motioned up to Sachin, his cargo handler. The other man murmured something and patted the railing before sagging against it, a grin on his face.

Earlier this morning, when Lune watched the only thing he owned in life towed in by the harbor patrol, both he and Sachin had to keep each other upright they'd been so panicked. Because the Jade Raptor was their livelihood. Their heart and soul. The boat's operation put food on the table, offered them freedom and adventure, and was Sachin's home. Except when there were terrible storms. Sachin would then tack up his hammock in Lune's room at the beach house.

Lune closed his eyes briefly, thanking the gods he'd convinced Sachin to sleep inland last night. It was always a challenge, as the Jade Raptor was as much Sachin's baby as it was his.

Most of the damage was topside. The main concern being the sail had been shredded by high winds and punishing waves. Lune knew he'd have to dip into his savings for the sail repairs. Or worse, he'd have to purchase a brand new one. Fingers crossed, it could be repaired. The construction and labor of that alone would set him back several more years. Force him back into a debt he just got out of. He'd only owned the Jade Raptor outright for two short months.

"She's strong, boss. She'll be up and running in no time. Leave it to me," Sachin offered anxiously. "I'll call in some favors, get the work prioritized. A week, tops."

His friend was trying to be upbeat. Sachin was the only employee he could afford—barely.

Lune plucked a coin from his purse and flipped it upwards with a splash. "Why don't you get back to your cabin and start re-organizing your stuff? Dinner's on me."

Sachin caught it. "Thanks. But I'll save that cleaning for tomorrow. I'm beat. Just going to grab some grub and then it's hammock time."

He'd offer to help tidy the inside, but Sachin was very prickly about his privacy. Lune respected that, despite being captain and sole owner of the Jade Raptor. The cabin was Sachin's home, and Lune would not enter unless invited, or if the boat was in danger of sinking.

"Night then." Lune was beat, too. There was nothing more desired than the need to face-plant himself in his bed.

"See ya bright and early, boss."

"Don't bother," Lune reminded. "You know how the sailmaker is after temple festivals. Especially the ones celebrating the undead phoenix god. He's not going to open until noon, at least."

"Grim's talons." Sachin complained with a good-natured sigh. "Oh well. That'll give me some extra sleep and time to set my room to rights. I'll knock at his door with strawberry pastries. They're finally in season."

"Don't forget black coffee." Lune laughed. "That'll get him out of bed."

"From the heavenly scent alone," Sachin agreed, before his voice went apologetic. "Uh...Lune? Thanks for ditching the festival this year. I know it means a lot to you."

"I wasn't about to let you sleep aboard without checking for damage below and beneath."

Lune meant it. The festival be damned. There was no way he was going to risk Sachin's life, even if his compass sparked at the festivals and lead him on a wild goose chase. A chase that came up empty each year. In the last few years, he'd figured it was standing on temple grounds that triggered the magical malfunction.

Sachin nodded before leaping over the boat railing to the dock. The initial downward momentum of Sachin's push-off dipped the Jade Raptor a few inches into the water, causing the boat to bounce drunkenly. Lune clutched at the hull. The impact of Sachin's boots hitting the dock made the structure tremble slightly as the cargo handler headed for the tavern for takeout.

Sputtering waves of water out of his mouth and wiping his eyes, Lune wondered at the sanity of befriending and hiring a half-gargoyle to toss luggage and manage difficult passengers. Especially when Sachin had been rejected by every other captain in the harbor.

When night fell, a gargoyle's skin naturally toughened up into a rocky texture and they tended to weigh more to reflect their earthen elemental ties. In that form, they took up a portion of a ship's maximum weight ratios that were meant for cargo or passengers. Gargoyles weren't buoyant in that form either, and that posed a fatal danger. But Jade Raptor was strong and welcomed Sachin well.

Lune swam for the dock ladder. In doing so, the current went warm. Squeezing his eyes shut, he prayed he wasn't wading through someone's urine. The harbormaster protected the cleanliness of her domain with an iron fist through her elemental powers. She also had her hands full keeping order among the pushy tourists who traveled through for the festival.

Grossed out, Lune heaved himself out of the water. He'd have to take a hot bath and maybe burn his clothes before retiring for the evening. But when the heat intensified and pressed against his hip bone, he realized.

Lune gasped. The warmth hadn't been some drunkard's piss; it emanated from his compass, and was getting hotter—but not enough to burn him. It surrounded him in a bright greenish glow. Gulping and attempting to breathe through both his mouth and gills in his elated shock, Lune steadied himself against the ladder's rungs.

The summons. His Intended. It was time.

Teary-eyed, Lune unhooked the compass from his belt and held it against his heart. He didn't know very much about his magical gift. Just the whispered rumors he'd eagerly absorbed over the years. That it would bring him joy and happiness. That he would find someone who understood him.

His wait was over.

His joy soon plummeted, and he clutched the compass tighter as the light quickly began to fade and die out. Until he was left with an inert compass, just like the one he woke up with this morning.

An urgency settled into his bones. As the light waned, the sense of his Intended also waned. A sick feeling in Lune's stomach rose. What was happening? Was his Intended hurt? Or sick?

The thirteen tiny green jewels surrounding the compass's bevel suddenly lit up. But he sensed it was not something to praise. It felt more like a warning.

One of the lights suddenly went dark.

An ominous, timed warning.

Further in a panic now, Lune hauled himself up the ladder and ran for home. Because if he needed time, then there was only one person he could trust to help.

Chapter 2

UPON THE CRAGGY ROCKS of the cliff-shore, Narsus of the Verdigris phoenix forge stood. Short of breath and a hand pressed against his pounding heart. The compass. A duty he spent his entire life trying to ignore now glowed. Summoning him to Temple Prime to wed. The very temple that rose high behind him. Where he himself had been hatched and raised.

To be in his phoenix form now would allow his emotions to run rampant and emote his grief, and thus spread the toxic nature of his poison phoenix heritage. So here he was, hiding in his human-self. Keeping the bitter feelings tamped down and somewhat under control. Even though they festered.

Since childhood, Narsus had been forever wrapped in the dark, heavy wool of his cloak and cowl. For added precaution, he'd included a scarf to cover his nose and mouth if need be. And a wide-brimmed hat to shadow his eyes. Not from the brilliance of the sunrises and sunsets he so loved, but to shield his view of the world that feared him and the harm he could do. To protect it from his poisonous nature. And so none could view his grief.

At his belt hung a pair of leather gloves, and his father's ominous, black-beaked mask. They were additional layers to guard those around him from the toxicity of his touch, his sweat, and from his very breath itself. The beaked mask was a temporary gift given until he could craft his own. But even Narsus shivered at the soulless stare of those large crystal lenses that made up the mask's eyes. Lenses darkened so his eyes weren't visible to those who gawked at him.

In reality, he didn't know if he had the courage to build his own mask. His template was so ominous, so menacing, that he was filled with hesitation. Unsure of where or how to even start. Or what design to pick.

Did he want to frighten the populace as his father did, to keep them at bay? Terrifying people wasn't kind. But he could not allow anyone near, lest they be harmed by his poisons.

Looped about Narsus's thin, quivering digits, was the chain of his compass. He pondered the destiny before him. And the reaction from the temple behind him should he refuse. In desperation and turmoil, his hands shifted. His dark emerald talons scraped against the glowing metal.

Pebbles crunched behind him. Narsus ignored Brightside's arrival, but pulled up the cloth scarf over his nose and mouth. Just in case.

"Your father just told me you never showed up to his not-hatchday festival," Brightside informed him. "I think you hurt his feelings. Your grandfather had to be a stand-in."

"I'll make it up to him next year." Narsus winced and tried not to think about the sorrow he'd caused over that. The guilt was digging in deep. He loved his father, but his compass would vibrate and buzz at each festival. Which meant his Compass-mate made the trek to Temple Prime every year to pay respects to the fire goddess, or to the undead phoenix god. Or both, as it was a joint celebration.

Every festival, Narsus would be on the move. Keeping one step ahead of the person frantically trying to track him. To have his mate that close, nearly within reach each year, was torture.

But this time, his compass had been silent. Narsus had been so depressed, he'd come to the cliff-side behind the temple to find some peace.

And attempt to reflect. To tell himself the Compass-alert had just been a magical malfunction.

Like it did when it had pointed to Cinder.

Narsus knew Brightside didn't understand the strife he felt at being Compass-born. Brightside wanted nothing more than to embrace his own Compass-destiny, but could not. The elf had lost his compass centuries ago in a shipwreck. Somewhere out there where Narsus now stared. Past the reefs and into the deepest depths of the ocean.

They were both broken and forgotten men, brought together by the darkness of woe and despair.

The sunset reflected in the waters, but the wind tugged at the scarf anchored about Narsus's neck. The element pushed back his hat instead, whipping his long green hair about in a frenzied halo. The color warned of his Verdigris phoenix heritage and the poison flowing through him, even in this human form. Absently, he tightened the hat strings so it would not be whisked away.

Narsus moved about restlessly upon the shadowy green flames that manifested beneath his magically protected boots. He looked out across the rolling waves, biting his lip so hard, blood trickled. It was followed by tears he blamed upon the cutting wind.

His Intended was calling out to him. Asking why he remained reticent.

He *had* to be silent. For the compass and its choice was wrong. Narsus had to do something, though. His Intended was on his way to Temple Prime. To him.

Narsus tried to pull his shoulders out of a sorrowful sag. Why now? Why now, after he'd already given up? There was nothing left. It was much too late. His heart was dead.

Anger suddenly raged along with the grief. Looking at the glowing, shimmering compass, the directional rose bobbed and slowly spun before stopping and pointing to the temple behind him. The one lone jewel that was burned out among its twelve shining companions mocked him. This compass was nothing but a burden. Additional reason to toss this cursed-filled heritage into the ocean and be done with it all.

So he did.

Brightside's soft gasp arose, and the elf took several hurried steps closer to the cliff. As if to try and rescue it, but failed, thankfully.

Narsus turned to his friend. "You have something to say?"

The elf's beautiful, usually neutral face was now pinched and angry. "When you formally asked me to bear witness, I—I seriously thought you'd changed your mind. I watched you register. You touched your compass to the assigned pairing stone, all for nothing?" He gestured toward the ocean. "You made a fool out of me. And yourself—twice, with this festival-disappearing fiasco. Why, Narsus? I don't understand."

"I didn't want to upstage my father, or the goddess, at their own celebrations by flashing around a glowing compass. I went through the marriage registration to keep the priests from harassing me."

Where Brightside's face had been twisted in anger, it now cast an edge of sympathy. "What you did for your father was noble, but he was still hurt you weren't at his side. Why are you denying yourself, and your Intended?"

"My Intended will be better off without me."

Brightside motioned again. "It didn't look that way before you threw away two lives. He was calling out to you. It glowed with joy. I've never seen a compass light up so strongly. Narsus, it's not too late. I can still see it, slowly sinking. Shift! Fly down and retrieve it. There, by the smaller log. Hurry!"

Narsus too, could see the bright cheery yellow gleaming out of the water from his peripheral vision. Phoenix eyes were just as sharp as an elf's. Instead, he turned to glare at the beautiful being beside him. "My

Intended will change their mind once they see I'm a poison phoenix. A dangerous Verdigris."

Narsus began to stride away on his cushion of flames. Only something made him pause. He forced himself not to look back into the water.

"It's gone," Brightside said softly. "I can no longer track it."

He knew. He'd felt it. Back still turned to his friend, Narsus dug his talons into his chest, cushioning the pain before he continued on toward the dark pit of misery he once called home. He was prepared for the many questions the priests would throw at him. Priests he grew up with. Priests who were relatives.

He yearned for his isolated mountaintop aerie. Away from the bustling population where there were no annoying priests to remind him of his magical compass heritage. Or that he was the son of the undead phoenix god. He turned to resume his escape.

"Nar!" Brightside rushed to block his path. But respectfully kept a wide distance between them. "You realize what you've done?"

"Yes. I've washed my hands of the honor." Narsus waved a hand in dismissal.

"Being Compass-born is a sacred duty," Brightside protested hotly. "To one's own heart. Our love and emotions help fuel and stabilize the magical gestalt bonds all priests, as well as Elementals, have with their paired anchors. Or have you forgotten that?"

Narsus asked himself if it was his imagination that Brightside's question held a note of fear. "Compass-borns are nothing but a backup source now," Narsus snapped. "At one time, I was elated to have this honor. But I was young and naive. Now, I would just taint the magic well with a broken heart. *A dead heart.*"

"Undead," Brightside corrected sharply. "My friend, you've deliberately isolated yourself. The courtesans have offered countless times—"

"That's *not* the kind of touch I want, Bree. Or yearn for."

"Punishing yourself over your triplex heritages—"

Narsus counted off on his fingers. "You think a Compass-born, undead, Verdigris is a blessing?"

Brightside carefully, slowly outstretched his arms. "I am wearing my long sleeves and gloves, as you can see."

Oh gods. An offered hug. From someone who cared about him. The corners of Narsus's mouth collapsed into a frown and his eyes stung. Before he could stop himself, his fire snapped out of existence. One shaky foot staggered over to the elf. Then the other joined in.

What was he doing? He'd almost caved. Brightside offered this embrace fairly often, but Narsus always rejected them out of fear of killing his best friend. It also felt *wrong* somehow. Like Narsus knew it wasn't what he needed in order to feel whole. That the act, no matter how honest, would leave him feeling even more miserable and empty.

Narsus spun away. "If there must be a marriage," he placated. "It can still be done because I've already registered."

"So you're opting for a very short marriage, then," Brightside clarified, heavy disapproval in the tone.

"Yes. Even without the compass, thirteen days will satisfy the requirements. Thirteen jewels on the compass bevel. Thirteen days to freedom for me, and the Intended."

Brightside's thin brows flattened. "But you still need to be there when your Intended shows up."

Being confined in a waiting room with strangers, and struggling to make sure he didn't harm anyone with his poisons, made Narsus shiver. The idea percolating in his mind cemented almost instantly. Brightside suddenly tensed.

Narsus knew the elf could see the intentions in his eyes. He held up a hand to bar his friend's protest. "You'll be there, Bree. Waiting for him.

As my proxy. Bring my Intended to me so we can put an end to this and send him on his way."

Brightside scowled. A strange sight on that elven face. "He'll know the instant I step into the marriage circle we don't belong together. What am I supposed to tell him?"

Narsus tried to set his shoulders up straight. "Tell him it's for his own protection. Because he's bound to a harmful, deadly—undead monster."

Chapter 3

LUNE BARRELED INTO THE beach house kitchen. Out of breath and dripping in sweat from his frantic sprint. Still clutching at his compass. At the little table, Calico spit out his tea, frazzled at the might of his chaotic arrival.

His father's guttural, accented voice exclaimed, "Now see here, my siren chick-peep—"

Wheezing and breathless from his run, all Lune could do was hold out the compass and shake it at the deity who'd raised him. The gods had created this magic. Calico must know how to fix it, know what was wrong with it.

"Oh! Marvelous. You have been called?"

Lune knew his thoughts were running rampant, but Calico was a telepath. Lune grunted, too excited to speak, but tried to focus enough to mentally communicate.

Calico jerked and gasped, dropping the tea towel he'd been using to mop up the spill. His father flapped his hands like a seal waving its flippers. Apparently, Lune's thoughts had been a little too jagged and rough. If he wasn't so distraught, he'd find it funny.

Centering himself, Calico got up and guided him to sit in the chair he'd just vacated. "Breathe, and settle, dear heart. Now, something is wrong with your compass?"

While he was calming down from the initial scare, it was easier to just think at his foster father. Lune squeezed his eyes shut and recalled the moment as he clung to the dock ladder. The surprising, acute joy slicing right into heartache and then instant confusion without any forewarning.

"There, there," Calico engulfed him in a hug. "No, I do not know what is wrong, or if there is truly anything amiss. With your Intended, or with the compass itself. I am not familiar with Compass-magic, nor do I know what the pulsing jewels mean."

Calico presented him with a glass of water. Lune took several short sips. Calico's mind hovered about his, lending quiet comfort until Lune let his shoulders sag.

"Thanks, Cal."

"Do you still sense a frightening urgency?"

Gritting his teeth, Lune paused to figure that out. And stared at his compass for additional support. No. He didn't feel anything. That was the problem. Before, there had always been a faint presence just out of his mental reach, but that was all.

"What does the compass say now?"

Lune lifted it and let the Compass-rose spin. "Pointing towards Temple Prime."

"Then you should prepare to go there."

Lune slumped in his chair, leaving the compass on the table. "Next boat for the main island goes out in the morning."

"Then you have plenty of time to have a repast, clean up, pack, and get some rest."

That sounded like a major chore, given that he still felt anxious and tense.

"A cup of tea to calm your nerves." The steamy brew was set next to Lune's water glass.

Lune snorted and disconnected himself from their telepathic conversation. His fingertips wrapped around the warm mug, further grounding his racing mind.

Taking a sip, Lune realized Calico had been at the Grim's festival. Bright purple paint covered Calico's face. The color signified Calico had gone to Temple Prime on the main island. The glittery paint slightly obscured the green and black filigree-like birthmarks that ran diagonally down each side of his foster father's face. There were also traces of purple powder dusted atop his half-shaved head and in his dark hair. It made the blue of his eyes stand out.

Magical birthmarks were an uncommon thing in the world, but enough magical folks had them that they weren't anything to be surprised about.

Lune pursed his lips and eyeballed his compass. Compass-borns also had birthmarks. His happened to be smack dab on his butt-cheek. When he'd been old enough to comprehend, Calico had given him a hand mirror. Then directed him to go into the privacy of his room to look at it.

His Compass-mark. On his ass. He imagined that somewhere out in the world, someone wore its match. Matching butt-cheeks. Charming.

"Sorry I missed the celebration," Lune said. "And seeing extended family."

"Nonsense. You had to rescue your boat. Is she any worse for wear?"

"Just the sail. Sachin'll have it fixed this week. Hopefully."

"That is very good to hear." Calico stood up, placing a hand against his shoulder. "Siren-peep? Lune."

Lune tensed, knowing what was coming. He wasn't ready to lose Calico. But his foster father was a wandering god. It was a parting they'd talked about in-depth for the last five years.

"The compass has called you. You have your own family now." Calico gave him a final pat and padded off to his room. Probably to pack.

Lune only sucked in a silent sob, and lay his head down on the table. It took a minute more to compose himself from the evening's turmoil. Then he got up and headed into his own room to prepare.

· ♥ · ♥ · ♥ · ♥ · ♥ ·

Lune washed. Scrubbed his body and wavy blond hair clean with the special soaps Calico highly recommended. The mixtures reeked of mango and elderberries.

His foster father had a thing for certain scents and flavors, because of his phoenix heritage. That included the delicious peppers Calico often prepared with their meals. The hotter the better his father declared, after bringing home seeds to plant in their garden.

Calico had collected several varieties during his travels throughout the realms, as he *was* the God of Space and Time. Calico called his favorite pepper plant *Carolina Reaper*. He had several other varieties dotted around their little garden, affectionately referring to them as *Ghost* or *Trinidad Moruga Scorpion*. Lune thought it odd Calico would name plants as if they were pets. His father had many endearing quirks.

Lune had to stop reminiscing and get to packing. He dug around in his chest of drawers for trousers without patches or frayed threads. To fill time, he'd even polished his leather boots and belt so they would complement his blue belt-sash. He'd wear a fresh tunic beneath the blue satin vest. It was the only set of formal garments he had. Over the years, Calico had tried to buy him more.

What did he need with fancy clothes when he steered a boat all day and handled luggage and cargo? When his love and life were riding the waves or racing beneath them. Or reveling in the ocean's cool breeze on the hottest of days.

By the time Lune was done packing, the sun had dipped below the horizon. He decided he would go sit out on the beach and try to relax. Listen to the waves crash against their private stretch of shoreline.

After years of waiting, Lune tried not to think of how nervous this magically-arranged fated mate marriage made him, even though he was eager for it. He'd gone back to the docks to explain to Sachin, but his friend was already snoring in his hammock. So he pinned a note to the cabin door, explaining.

The compass's light flickered, drawing Lune's attention. Although not as vibrant as it was a few hours before. That lone, unlit jewel among its brighter siblings made his stomach flop.

"What happened, my Intended?" he asked of the magical metal. "Where did you go?"

The evening embracing the landscape was so very cozy and romantic. But not having anyone to share it with lay heavy on his heart. Over the years, he'd had long, one-sided conversations with his compass. Sometimes, he almost thought he sensed affection radiating from it. Although lately, it felt as if no one was on the other side anymore.

The heavenly smell of vanilla waffles drifted from the beach house's kitchen, breaking Lune from his thoughts. Vanilla was a very special treat. Waffles were usually served flavored of cayenne pepper or cinnamon. Calico always said waffles were the most magical of dinners. Lune agreed, especially if there was Calico's homemade strawberry syrup and the honey harvested from the apiary about a mile down the road.

Magical. A word, and a craft he'd grown up with, but personally knew so little about. Calico wove magic so often into their day-to-day life, and talked about it so much, maybe Lune had just taken it for granted.

Lune sighed, unhooking the compass that was attached to his belt. The few times he'd drilled Calico for information about it, his phoenix-born foster father always said if he had questions, he would need to trek to a temple.

Holding the compass aloft by its chain, Lune studied the silver casing. The calm rush of ocean waves lapping against the sand lulled him into further reflection.

The glossy compass face was the shade of aged paper; its directional rose-star cast in a deep, metallic black. Thirteen verdant jewels decorated the bevel—his anxious gaze skipped over the one that had winked out.

This Compass-union was the chance to start a new life. To connect with someone. To grow and learn from each other. Laugh with each other. And, Lune hoped, to someday fall in love with. That lifelong support was something he yearned for. Because he'd been shown love and guidance by the strange, wayfaring god who'd raised him since birth.

Lune smirked with affection. Calico was...how would Calico put it...? An odd kettle of fish? An eccentric old bean? His smirk soon turned to wistfulness. He'd miss his father.

He glanced over his shoulder. Through the window, Calico tucked dust blankets over the furniture, and packed up food to distribute to the neighbors. The tiny two-bedroom beach house they'd called home was being closed up.

It was often custom for newlyweds—especially fated mates or arranged marriages—to spend their honeymoon getting to know each other on neutral ground. Then decide where they wanted to go from there. And the city below Temple Prime was *the* place to hang out while making that decision. Or so Lune had heard from friends.

Calico had tried to reassure him that this wasn't the end. That they'd see each other again. Someday. But someday was an eternity.

Lune stood up, brushing the sand off his trousers. He followed the delicious scent of waffles to its origin. There, in their beach house kitchen, his father's presence lit up the room.

The friendly warmth of Calico's phoenix-self radiated around his portly, human form. He looked to be in his early 50s, with a big, round belly hiding behind the long chef's apron. A white scarf concealed his half-shaved head, and his dark hair was bound into a queue down his back. Calico's eyes currently beamed with tranquility, but the stress-wrinkles of an old, unspoken turmoil still marred them.

"My siren-chick is leaving the nest." Calico retrieved a linen from the pocket of his floor-length skirt and dabbed at his tears. "This will be the last meal I shall cook for you."

As usual, Calico enunciated all his words with utmost care. Lune knew his father was native-born to this realm, but entwined within those deep, guttural tones was the hint of a very strange accent. One he'd not heard in his years of ferrying visitors and foreigners all around the archipelago.

"I shall be away, procuring your wedding present," Calico said. "But I will return in plenty of time for the actual ceremony."

"Cal, I told you. I don't need anything. You being there is more important."

"Of course I must find you a wedding present. What sort of father and mentor would I be if I did not? Now come and eat your dinner before the waffles go cold."

Lune sat at the table and fiddled with the small pot of strawberry syrup. "Why aren't you coming with me?"

Calico laughed. "You have not needed your daddy to hold your hand since you were thirteen. Besides, solo travel builds character and confidence."

Calico did have a point. Other than his one failed attempt to travel alone when he came of age. His father slid another waffle onto his plate, then pat his shoulders before dropping a kiss against his forehead. "No sulking. Eat."

Lune drowned the treat in butter and strawberry syrup. Then savored the faint scrape of the knife across the golden crust. He wasn't sulking. He was in mourning. It had just been him and Calico for so long.

He grasped for grounding happy memories. Sachin popped up around his thirteenth birthday. Just when he'd gotten his hands on the junker he'd renamed the Jade Raptor. Together, he and Sachin fixed her up and made her shine again. At least Sachin would remain a familiar constant in his life.

Calico sat beside him, pouring a generous amount of syrup on his own breakfast. "You still fear what being away from the water that long will do."

Lune nodded, subdued.

"Well," Calico said with a cheerful wink. "My magic will fix that. I have re-spelled your scarf to keep your gills hydrated for the duration of your honeymoon journey."

"Thanks."

"Things will work out, my siren-peep. Have faith."

"That's what's worrying me." Lune grimaced, mopping up the last bit of syrup with the last bite of waffle. Calico leaving was just a small spiral to his mood that he couldn't stop thinking about. But what overshadowed that was the continued strange disconnect from his Intended.

Chapter 4

Morning greeted Lune with a second burnt-out jewel, and growing anxiety.

When he stepped out of his room, though, the beach house felt different. Cold. He knew Calico was gone. They'd said their goodbyes last night.

Setting his shoulders back, he knew it would take a measure of adjustment to get used to. Instead, there was a new joy on the horizon to soften the melancholy.

Today was the first day of starting a future with his Intended. Lune grabbed fruit on his way out the door. Squinting at the glowing rays of the rising sun, he hurried to the docks.

The boat to the main island was twice as big as his Jade Raptor, and powered by magic to shorten travel time. The decks and lounges allowed just enough space to stroll and pace without bumping into too many passengers.

Twenty minutes into the inter-island journey, Lune realized he'd been avoiding the guard rails and views of the ocean. Once, when he was diving with Cal beyond the reef for a tenth birthday present, a shark had grabbed him. Calico had acted quickly, with the blind rage of any divine being or magic-wielder protecting its young. The thing had been boiled alive—under water, and there hadn't been a trace of any flame.

They'd feasted on the meat for the rest of the week and had enough to share with the neighbors. Lune rubbed at the shark-toothed scars on his arm and then fiddled with the scarf around his neck. Calico's magic curling around the hemp fabric kept his gills hydrated, so his breathing was easy. Although, being so far away from home, even though it was the archipelago—out near the open ocean—instilled low-level anxiety.

A couple of short horn blasts signaled their arrival. Dock workers scrambled along a narrow pier carved into the rock face. They helped the crew moor the boat. Passengers pushed and shoved, queueing up to disembark. Lune loitered to be the last to leave. He didn't look forward to staring at someone's arse, or someone staring at his, as he climbed the ladders anchored into the cliff-side.

Temple Prime sat on the high cliff. It was built that way back in the ancient days. For defense. Now that the gods were just about all at peace with each other, a more direct route had been constructed for the impatient. The only other way to visit Temple for those who didn't fly or have some sort of magical transportation, was a full day walk from the harbor.

Coming here as a child and a youth for festivals had been fun and easy. Calico just shifted into his phoenix form, and Lune had flown in on his father's back. As Lune got older, taller, and heavier, an aging Calico opted to use his dimensional portal for their transport. While Lune reveled in the immediate convenience of the god-magic, his childhood self missed the breath-taking views of their Star Land Island archipelago.

But he was no longer a child. He was here to be married. To his fated mate.

Once at the temple gates, Lune was able to bypass the lines and security measures by showing his compass to the guards. He got through the inner ward just fine, but at the offices, it took several hours of interviews and paperwork before he was allowed upstairs.

From there, he was met with a Blue Robed priest who escorted him to private quarters. Rules of his stay, and of the marriage ceremony itself, were repeated with pleasant and engaged interest. When Lune asked about his Intended, he was told his mate was sequestered in meditation. That the ceremony would take place at sunrise, before breakfast.

Which meant Lune would be awake all night, pacing in anticipation. Wondering if his match was a priest. Because of the mention of meditations. That would fit being unable to find him during festivals. Priests were always so busy, especially then.

When the rooster's call pierced the dawn, he was escorted into the waiting hall. A few dozen priests and other people were already mingling.

Clutching at his compass, Lune let his gaze flit over them, wondering who among them was his match. About four other Compass-bearers were present and engaged in animated conversations with both the Blue, and Green Robed priests.

Lune felt nothing as he studied his peers, and his compass remained extinguished. Instead, his attention was drawn to the tall, thin silhouette lingering in the corner shadows. He was unable to get a good look because of the brilliant sunrays that flooded the hall. So he approached.

Closer now, the details emerged. The man's tall, lean body was dressed smartly in ash-gray trousers and a long-sleeved tunic. The material was clearly of the highest quality. Light not only bounced off the faintly glowing compass at the man's waist, but lured Lune's attention upward.

Lune swallowed a shriek, lest he bring attention to himself.

The metallic winged helmet paired with a face shield meant he was a cockatrice in human form. The clear, lemon-yellow tinted glass was created out of magic to negate that deadly stare.

Gulping, Lune started forward again, compass in hand.

What the avian serpent-shifter did next shocked Lune. The mysterious man turned his back with a smooth, slow, and deliberately controlled spin.

Lune was being told a firm *no*. He was not to approach. Lune halted, confused. To push the issue would be a social calamity. A grave and unforgivable insult that could ruin reputations.

Biting his lip and slightly hunching his shoulders in embarrassment, Lune casually wandered back in the opposite direction. When priests came for him, Lune tried to stall as he quickly scanned the hall for Calico. His father had promised to attend. But priests ushered him along into one of several wedding chambers.

An empty chamber.

Lead up to a simple altar and abandoned, Lune wiped sweaty hands on his vest. The quiet of the small room was loud in his ears. He glanced at the glowing stone perched atop a squat, nondescript pedestal. Lune let himself get lost in the gently pulsing light. He'd been told his Intended had presented his own compass days ago, which was the reason for the glow. Lune's half of the stone was dark, awaiting magical activation.

Low voices were at the door. Lune sucked in a breath.

Someone entered. Their stride was well-trod and full of confidence. Just like the cockatrice. That increased Lune's nervous sweat, and his delight.

Lune deliberately didn't look at his Compass-match until his Intended stood before him. Because he wanted those extra precious few seconds to not make another fool of himself.

This was it. When he lifted his head, Lune was rendered speechless. Where was the cockatrice?

Lune swallowed another breath and felt the flush of heat on his cheeks. This elf was gorgeous—almost hypnotically so. Tall and svelte. Gentle angles and curves. Sparkling green eyes like emeralds and silver-white hair cut in feathery wisps reached past his shoulders. Pale skin. The detailed finery of his clothing held a faint glittery texture, and Lune suspected that this elegance *was* his everyday wear.

This was his Intended? Clearing his head of the distraction, Lune realized the elf wasn't carrying a compass. Before he could inquire, the Blue Robed priest motioned for Lune to touch his compass upon the magical crystal. He did, and the rock glowed, signaling a match.

The rest of the ceremony itself was a blur. Lune was transfixed by his Intended's cool and aloof beauty. But that was only skin-deep. He wanted to hear that voice, see some measure of emotion, a reaction, light up his fated mate's face.

The priest bowed to them, and departed.

"Are you ready to leave?" the elf asked coolly. "Or do you need to collect luggage from your room?"

Broken from the trance of beauty, Lune took that second to scan the elf's belt, then around his neck. He wasn't carrying a compass. At least not in view. Lune frowned and checked his own apparatus.

It wasn't glowing now, and neither was the marriage stone upon the altar. That was something the priests hadn't covered in the wedding orientation. Or had they? So much new information had been thrown at him, it'd been impossible to absorb it all at once.

"I'm Lune." He held out his compass. It still did not glow. "It's wonderful to finally meet you. But I'm confused. Where's yours?"

"Did they not tell you? I am merely the proxy." The elf rolled up his sleeve, revealing a compass birthmark upon his lean biceps. It in no way matched his.

Lune blinked. "P-proxy?"

"Yes. Narsus sent me in his stead."

"Narsus?"

"Your Intended," the elf replied. "My name is Brightside."

"Oh. Right. Of course." But it wasn't right. This had to be a mistake of some sort. It was a full minute before Lune could form a coherent sentence. "Why...why didn't he come?" Then the worry surfaced—he recalled the silence from his compass as he talked to it. Lune took an urgent step, hands pressed around his compass, as if to soothe himself. "Is he okay? Is he hurt?"

"Narsus will have to explain these arrangements," was the only answer provided. "He waits at the edge of the city."

The elf strode elegantly from the chamber with the same self-assuredness as when he'd entered. Leaving Lune to urgently follow.

·♥·♥·♥·♥·♥·

Brightside led him through Temple Prime's dual courtyards, all the way across the city, and out into the wilds before slowing down. Having to meet his mate in the middle of nowhere was wrong and insulting. And certainly a bit disconcerting.

Being left at the altar without any explanation was infuriating. This elf would have told him if Narsus was sick, or injured, wouldn't he? Lune tried to keep his temper, but it wavered between concern and annoyance. With each step, he became more riled. Especially since Brightside was not the type for idle chatter.

A defensive spell flashing in warning snapped Lune out of his thoughts and left spots in his eyes. Brightside crowded up in front of him. As if to protect. Brilliant blue light danced around the elf's hands, and Lune could sense the leashed destruction should the magic be shot forward. He tensed, and let the elf handle the situation.

Lune knew how dangerous magic could be from his father. Calico had also warned him of thieves, especially out on isolated country roads. Especially of pickpockets in the towns and cities.

30

Scanning for the danger, Lune found it. The cockatrice again. He was leaning up against a tree. Watching intently. His glowing compass dangling leisurely from his fingertips.

When Brightside's spell grew even more luminous in defense, the avian serpent-shifter again turned his back, permitting them to be on their way.

What in Nolth's underworld realm was going on? Was the cockatrice just bored, waiting around for his fated mate to show up? Or did he just want to be a stalking creep? Lune was relieved his escort was deemed enough of a threat to deter any trouble.

Brightside grabbed Lune's arm and escorted him past the other Compass-bearer. Then kept checking back to make sure they weren't being followed. Walking over the hill, the elf glanced at him for the first time since leaving the temple.

"We're here." Brightside pointed toward the edge of the forest.

Lune made out a dark, shrouded figure, also loitering beneath the canopy of a big, leafy tree. Seeking shade was a common activity here in the Star Lands because of the excessive heat.

His fated mate was tall. The mask worn—Lune prayed it was a mask—was matte black, and sported a large beak. The eye holes were covered in convex shiny black crystal lenses the size of oranges.

Lune grunted, and wobbled in confusion and fright. *The mask! This was the mask of the undead phoenix god.* Lune's labored breathing had Brightside reaching for his elbow to hold him up. The touch shattered Lune's shock, and logical thinking kicked in.

No. The Grim god wasn't his mate. His Intended had just adopted the trademarked mask. A mask that wasn't even used by the populace during festivals. Because it was a sacred item. So why was Narsus wearing it?

This day was growing stranger and more stressful by the minute. Where was his father? He needed a friendly, familiar face about now.

31

Lune put a fist against his mouth and stared. When Narsus seemed to twitch at the scrutiny, Lune took out his compass to confirm his silent query. The directional Compass-rose lit up and pointed directly to Narsus. It had never shone this intensely before. The birthmark on his ass felt warm, as if it too, had lit up.

Lune gasped when Narsus glided out of the shadows. *Glided.* On curling tendrils of multi-green flames. Those flames, flailing beneath boots that didn't burn. It was as if there was a thin layer of air that buffered the fire.

When paired with the bird mask, it was starting to make sense.

Was Narsus a phoenix? An undead phoenix, by the looks of him. Or was he one of Grim's high priests, by evidence of the mask? No. Not even Grim's sacred servants wore such a mask.

Lune couldn't be sure of any of this without more evidence, even though he was raised by a phoenix. There were one or two other phoenix forges native to the island archipelago, and their population was strong. But the green-flamed Verdigris was not one of them.

As Lune approached, trying to get a better look at his mate, the sun shone down on that towering figure, casting greater shadows within the folds of that cloak and mask. The effect made Narsus more fluid than before. More scary. Especially when his mate retreated into the dappled shade at his advancement.

Lune squared his shoulders. Even by the middling distance between them, Narsus was at least a foot and a half taller. With each step Lune took, Narsus took two steps back. So Lune backpedaled, halting the perceived aggression. If Narsus was the nervous sort, he didn't want to brand himself as domineering and pushy.

It was unfortunate the priests or even Brightside hadn't provided him with Narsus's proper title of address. The morning sun highlighted the metallic rivets of that black-beaked mask. Made the shadows cast upon it deeper, with more texture. Lune didn't know whether to stay terrified, or find comfort in what was his husband.

So he would do what his father would do. He bowed, but only slightly. "Hello, Narsus. I'm Lune. I'm very pleased to be here. To meet you. Even at this unusual method of introduction."

Great gods, he was starting to babble, to talk like Calico.

Lune was insulted at the way his husband's shoulders drooped. Was he that lacking, while Narsus hid himself from the same judgment?

This marriage was already off to a very poor start. The negative response prompted Lune to close the compass lid and hook it back onto his belt. That immediately prompted the towering mountain to slowly walk around Lune. The beaked mask bent in study. As if making sure he wasn't the one who was a fraud.

Narsus pulled back his cloak and motioned to his trousered backside. Muffled by that leather mask, he said, "Neither of us will be dropping our pants for a birthmark confirmation."

Lune's heart skipped with joy. A gentleman. Maybe this could work out after all. Narsus was just as nervous as he was.

"You'll do."

Lune's eagerness plummeted, causing him to hold tight to his shock and not let it slip away. Those rumbled words assaulting his ears almost made him lose his temper.

"I'll do?" Lune asked, going numb. His hurt reflected upon those glass lenses set into that ugly mask. "I'll do?" he asked again. His fingers dug into his compass as he clenched at it.

There was a round of deliberate coughing and throat clearing from Brightside. Lune had forgotten the elf was here. Apparently, so had Narsus. That mask turned toward the elf, but then soon dismissed him. Lune gulped when he felt the full, pressing weight of Narsus's concealed stare.

"Time to go." Narsus turned and walked away.

What to do? What was there to do? Lune contemplated his options as Narsus got farther and farther away with each step.

Brightside seemed torn. He followed Narsus for a few steps, stopped, then turned and looked at him. The elf shrugged in elegant apology and followed Narsus. Brightside kept looking back. Pausing to see if he'd come. Then hurried on.

Narsus did neither.

That struck another nerve. It wasn't like Lune expected his new husband to fall all over him and confess undying love. But showing some respect, even the tiniest measure was expected. Maybe even a hint of interest would've been nice.

Faint echoes from the city's marketplace reached Lune's ears, helping him regain the sense of his surroundings. Narsus and Brightside were gone. He'd been so out of it he hadn't noticed there were two separate roads.

Which one had they traveled? Lune stood there and waited another ten minutes. Hoping that maybe Narsus just had a case of nerves. Like he had. In reality, he knew it had been ten minutes too long.

Did he really want to have a mate—*a fated mate*—who had so little regard for him?

No, he didn't.

Calico once said the compass magic wasn't infallible. That there were mistakes. Hiccups in the magic because it was the first of its kind. Calico knew that much because of his affiliation with other gods. But that was his father's extent of compass lore.

Why should Lune give someone a chance who showed him so little respect and interest? And if he did try to follow Narsus, and found him on the trail, how would the balance of the relationship work out in the long run? Would he forever be striving to please Narsus at the expense of himself? Would he lose himself, and thus lose his own self-respect? Would he learn he didn't matter as he continued to seek Narsus's approval? Narsus said it himself. He'd do. He was nothing but baggage to the poison phoenix.

Lune felt a heavy sting in his jaw as he held back the tears that threatened to leak. The more he thought about it, the more sorrow blanketed his heart. There was no chance Narsus would ever love. This phoenix wasn't even in possession of his compass. As Calico would say, this was the final red flag.

Was this why Calico hadn't shown up? Had he known?

Taking a deep breath, Lune wiped wet eyes against his sleeve. Stubbornly, he forced himself to wait another several minutes. Several minutes turned into thirty.

Narsus wasn't coming back.

Thirty minutes sacrificed out of a lifetime. A lifetime of emotional neglect averted. That told Lune all he needed to know. He turned and headed back to the docks.

To his beach house home.

"Narsus, will you slow down?" Brightside rushed to catch up. "He's not following."

"He'll come."

Brightside rolled his eyes and huffed. "Your mask needs to be defogged. How could you read him that wrong? I think your own doubts got in the way. Your Intended was furious. You can't keep treating people this way. Or yourself."

Narsus snarled.

"I don't understand you," Brightside admonished. "I'll never get my compass back. It's gone. Rotted at the bottom of the ocean. I'd give anything to have a second chance, to have a Compass-heart at my side. I know how much the loneliness kills you. You're throwing away your chance at happiness."

Verdant flame flared, coiling and curling up beyond Narsus's height. Narsus knew his friend was too used to the whipping flames to be scared. "I'm the one who can't touch anyone, Bree, not you. I'm the one who can't let anyone close."

"You're making a big mistake to not even try," Brightside said quietly.

"I have tried," Narsus replied just as low. "It ended in grief and tears. Enough. I don't want to hear anymore."

Narsus turned away, and his cloak billowed. Verdant magic glittered and glowed. His clothing and gear morphing, being tucked away into an unseen mystical dimension that served as a pocket. Then his human form also faded. In its place was a whirling funnel of green flame that transformed into a brilliant, long-tailed phoenix. Narsus launched his stocky, rooster-shaped body into the air and flew away on broad, fiery wings.

Chapter 5

EVEN AFTER A FULL day of traveling, Lune was still angry. Confused. He slammed the door of the little beach house, and fell into a chair facing the ocean. His head lolled back. The tired ache radiating from his bones finally hit him, and he slumped further. If he wasn't so exhausted, mentally and physically, he'd go for a swim. Despite the magic scarf around his neck, he needed the touch of genuine water. To reconnect himself back into the natural elements. Maybe he could just flop around in the surf and watch the stars.

From his peripheral vision, there was a note propped up on the kitchen table. He dragged himself up to fetch it. The key to Calico's bedroom was attached.

My dearest siren chick peep,

Being the God of Space and Time, of course I knew you would come home. No judgment. I raised you to think for yourself, to protect yourself and your mental wellness, but also to have compassion for others—but not at your personal expense.

I apologize for not attending the formalities of your proxy. It can be devastatingly disheartening when first impressions do not hold up to proper expectations. But give it a chance, for you have not even gotten started. I understand your discord, as I too, have had strife with my own chosen mate. At the moment, my estranged ex-husband and I are in a very delicate truce.

Over what I shall not reveal. I will only say that he broke my heart to the point I was certain I could never forgive or return to the pairing, despite it being a celestially destined match.

Finding you, raising you, has been such a joy to me, and I thank you for allowing me to be in your life. You have healed a wound inside my soul, and helped me to reflect. If I can grant this relationship with my ex-husband one last chance, allow him this one last chance to prove himself, will you not consider your own?

Love, Calico

Calico was married? That was a huge surprise. It was likely the reason his father had started wandering again in the last year or two. Perhaps even visiting this mysterious ex-husband Lune had never known about.

Lune wasn't too surprised though, that Calico had already known of the proxy. He should've realized that on the way home. Because Calico was the physical embodiment of Time itself.

As a child, he never could hide anything from his father. Calico knew before Lune even realized he wanted to lie about skipping school to dive off cliffs and explore underwater caves.

Still, he'd always miss Calico's company. But as the letter stated, he was attempting to work on his own marriage. It surprised him Calico had even been in a relationship, as he'd never talked about it before. With a smile, Lune wondered what type of person had caught his father's eye, but soon put that thought aside. He had his own turmoil to deal with.

Or not.

Despite Calico's advice, Lune wouldn't take it. Not this time. Why should he put his heart and his energy into someone who considered him a bother and an inconvenience? He folded the note and placed it in his pocket for safekeeping.

He couldn't help sneak a look at his compass though. The two jewels encircling the bevel were still out. Lune froze at the odd feeling he got from it. Then shrugged and stuffed it in his pocket so he wouldn't be reminded.

To busy himself and keep his mind off his failed Compass-marriage, Lune fussed around the beach house. It was so depressing to have to go around and pull off all the dust dropcloths and fold them for storage. There was also no food in the pantry—he should've remembered. He found that out the hard way, after the sun had set. Digging through all the cupboards came up empty. It would be highly embarrassing to ask the neighbors for something to get him through the night.

The cast iron waffle mold wasn't in the pantry. That depressed Lune more. He'd been hoping to have a silly little lifeline to some trivial comfort. So he'd just sit here and suffer until morning, watching the waves and questioning his sanity, wondering if he'd made the right decision. Lune snorted. Of course he had!

His stomach growled. Right now, he lamented the loss of waffles more than a selfish, dense, haughty asshole of a Compass-husband.

Water was the only thing to fill his belly with, but he didn't look forward to the sloshy bloat as he lay here and stewed. He really should have swung by the market during his trek, but he'd been too wrapped up in his fuming. The merchants had been closing up for the evening anyway, anxious to get home themselves.

Suddenly, he blinked as the realization dawned. Calico's bedroom. It had always been off limits. He didn't even know what it looked like inside. He'd tried once or twice as a youth, but the door was magically locked, and he had no such ability.

He wondered... Well, at least it would make for a distraction from his hunger. Lune lunged to his feet, grabbed the key, and stopped before the door. His heart was already pounding. Eager curiosity got the best of him. He touched the doorknob and there was no magical push back. He inserted the key and pushed the door open.

A gentle whiff of cinnamon tickled his nose. The room was a pale cheery blue with plank board walls and white trim. The bed was big, neatly made, and covered with a plain blue blanket. A little blackened pipe stove was clean and well-used. A fitting accessory for a phoenix.

Twinkling crystals hung from the ceiling and near the large circular window that took up the entire wall—a window that had privacy spells upon it so that you couldn't look in from the other side. He blushed, remembering. Calico had cast that magical curtain when Lune had been old enough to start snooping.

The view from the big, round window let in as much light as possible, and faced the tide pools where Lune had spent his years as a fry.

A small section of the garden was also visible. It had always been lovely, full of flowers and fresh vegetables. When Calico lived here, he'd always be out working in the garden or baking in the kitchen. Lune knew the garden was currently stripped and spent, because he'd helped Calico close out this particular growing cycle just a few days ago.

Lune shook out the yearning for the harmony he'd grown up with. He resigned himself to the fact that his Compass-mate hadn't been a match after all.

A plate of food on the corner nightstand caught his eye. Dried meat, cheese, and crackers were an eager delight. There was another note with his name on it, tented upon the cheese wedge.

Lune chuckled. Calico knew him too well. Walking across the planked floor, he picked up the paper.

Hello again, my siren child.

I have removed anything dangerous or magical from this suite—even the spells upon the window—but not its magical fire-proofing. You will probably need that.

I knew you could not resist sneaking a peek at my private abode. You are free to use this space as your own, for the beach house is now yours. The updated deed is filed at the town hall. A fitting wedding present, as I will not be returning anytime soon after all.

In the meantime, I could not let my boy go hungry. So here is a snack to get you through the night, and some currency to carry your meals through the week. Consume wisely, for after that, you are on your own.

Love, Calico

P.S. Yes, I have taken my waffle iron pan home with me. Agustin enjoys waffles just as much as you do.

Ah! The mysterious, estranged ex-husband had a name. Lune folded up the notes before inserting both of them in a drawer for safekeeping. Too bad about the waffle pan confirmation. He could've gone for some of Calico's strawberry and honey waffles about now, but the small meal Calico had left more than satisfied his belly.

It was also only fair to share the treat with this Agustin. The poor fellow had been deprived of Calico's waffles for twenty years, at least—Lune felt his face turn beet red. Dammit, his mind just had to dive off into the gutter. He gave his head a shake to reset himself. Because he loved waffles too much to associate it with a double entendre.

Even though Calico taught him how to be self-sufficient, if Lune did make the treat for himself, it wouldn't be the same. Not to mention the ingredients were expensive here on the farthest island. He'd be living on what he could catch from the ocean, but he *and* his stomach had grown too accustomed to human food.

Sitting around twiddling his thumbs would give him too much time to overthink as the days passed. Getting right back into work would help. Because there'd been yet another headache waiting for him. When he'd disembarked from the ship that had brought him home, he'd swung by to talk to Sachin.

The Jade Raptor wasn't anchored in her slip, or in the repair cove. He'd have to check in with the harbormaster to pin down Sachin's whereabouts. Lune wasn't too worried yet. His friend knew the beach house was always a haven, and the gargoyle didn't need to ask permission for somewhere to lay his head.

Lune took a second glance around Calico's former quarters. The closet was surprisingly a space he could walk into. Inside was a small writing desk, and rows of empty shelves. Propped up against the wall was a long piece of wood about as tall as him. It had notches at both ends.

It was a bundling board.

He *had* been in this suite before! Lune remembered that now. When he was very small. The plank had been hooked into the bed's header and footer. Calico used it during Lune's nightmare phase—to keep Calico from being sliced to pieces as Lune wailed and cried that the predator fish in the ocean were attacking him, chasing him.

Lune paled. He flipped the bundling board around. Tiny, child-sized claw marks were gouged in the wood. He shook the flood of memories loose. It was a shock that he'd even gotten back into the water after those night terrors. But Calico had also helped with that. Letting him swim around and play in the big bathtub for as long as he wanted. Then returning to the tide pools before graduating back into the ocean.

That also brought back the memories of Calico gently shushing him as a toddler, every time he felt happy enough to sing. Sometimes, Calico urged him with gentle inquiries to adjust his tone, usually when he was too happy. Calico assured him it was just his nature. And that his song should be tempered for the safety of others, not shut away. It was unfortunate that the instruction never took hold, for Lune still sang or hummed from time to time.

The once-lost memory gripped him. Lune tensed up enough that he had to grip the door frame to steady himself. As a child, during their many swim lessons, he'd nearly drowned Cal on several occasions with his siren's singing. Immediately, he shook the once-fogged memory out of his head.

Taking a deep breath, Lune exited the closet and strode over to another closed door. Yes, it was the spacious, private washroom. The bath consisted of a nice tub that could be a small tidal pool. In another enclosed alcove, at the far side of the room, there was a toilet.

This place was fit for a king. No...a god, just as Calico was.

Lune decided to fill the tub for a good long soak. As he did, he couldn't help but think back and wonder if he could have handled the encounter with Narsus any better.

But as he dried off and headed for bed, doubts surfaced. No. He'd made the right decision, and the gentle crashing of the waves outside confirmed it. He was home. This is where he belonged. With the Jade Raptor. And sailing his local routes with Sachin.

Only, some small part of him still obsessed over Narsus. Of how his Intended had carried himself. That mysterious and aloof mood, further enhanced by his slightly terrifying appearance. The deepness of that muffled voice...

Lune grabbed a pillow and shoved it over his head, trying to shut out the disruptive thoughts. And failed.

Chapter 6

Narsus had visited Brightside's abode several times over the years. It was so different from the unorganized chaos of his own aerie. His friend's home was welcoming and whimsical. A cross between farm life and forest living. Earthy tones and natural elements were abound, accented by various polished stones, seashells, dried as well as fresh botanicals, and all wood furniture.

But so very, very cold here in the high mountains. Brightside's hearth was an open-ended contraption that heated the entire cottage. Without spells or magic.

Here in the kitchen, plants and shiny bits of crystal shards nestled in nooks, catching the light peppering through windows that were shaded by the trees outside. Books stacked neatly on shelves contained recipes for food, healing, and magic—so different from Grandfather's slightly chaotic collections.

Brightside never claimed or considered himself to be a witch. Or even a wizard, like Calico. His friend just said he *was*. Encouraging the natural energies, the gifts, and interests that manifested before him and around him. While Brightside never said, Narsus suspected he was only half-elf, and the rest of his bloodline was nature-based. Of the very verdure itself.

Narsus had always enjoyed his time here. Until now. Because the elf blasted him with that infamous stare-of-judgment while peeling an orange. All without lowering his gaze to the said peeling. The discarded rinds were left neatly stacked on an empty dinner plate.

They'd just finished supper, but Brightside had a sweet tooth and insisted on dessert. And unfortunately, conversation. "So you're going through with ignoring your new husband?"

Narsus glared, his feet up on another chair, and too full to properly argue. "Compass-husband."

"There's a difference?" Brightside blinked with surprise.

"Of course there isn't," Cinder declared, breezing in from where ever he'd been in the house. The dust wand in his hand never stopped moving as he went about his task.

Cinder was a phoenix of the Cottage Forge. And, unfortunately, a Compass-born, too. There were certain behaviors Cinder wouldn't let Narsus get away with. Both of the Compass-kind, and of the phoenix-kind.

Which was why Brightside had trekked all the way to Narsus's bleak and isolated cabin. Then coaxed him to spend a few days in cozier surroundings.

Neither man never let him wallow for long. They didn't tolerate it. In reality, the three of them had been dear friends for ages, and Narsus was very happy to have them in his life. Even when he was mentally immersed in his darkest moments.

Cinder had always been Brightside's secret weapon against him. Even before the trauma of the ill-fated Compass-match Narsus had had with the Cottage phoenix. And most especially after the said trauma.

The parting between him and Cinder had been...grievous.

But Cinder no longer knew that.

Narsus glared at the other phoenix fluttering about. Cinder had been waiting and ready for them with lots of food. And direct conversations.

Narsus fumed. What would Grandfather Calico call this? An intervention?

Cinder cheerfully ignored him, his dancing orange eyes kindling with mischief. A kerchief kept his riot of orange-reddish curls out of his face, and there were smudges of ash on his cheeks from cleaning out the hearth—which was his ultimate favorite task. Sleeping in the fire pit was one of Cinder's most favorite things to do—as a flame among the flames.

To be fair, most phoenix partook of that pastime—when in clandestine surroundings. Which reminded Narsus that maybe Brightside knew more about phoenix than he let on. It also made him wonder if the friendship between Brightside and Cinder was more intimate than they let on. But that was none of his business.

"What was wrong with your Intended?" Brightside pressed. "He was cute! Very open to meeting his fated mate. Sun-kissed with sun-bleached hair, too."

"Of course there's nothing wrong with his Intended!" Cinder declared. The dust wand in his hand never stopped moving. "Narsus is just being a deliberate ass, trying to protect himself."

Narsus continued to glare at Cinder. Cinder, who self-appointed himself to be Bree's live-in housekeeper. Because he was bored. And anticipating his own Compass-call. He said it would be soon, as he could feel it in his bird-bones.

Narsus took a gulp of his drink. In reality, Cinder had lived with Brightside since...the incident. It was always hard for Narsus to visit here, but he kept doing so.

Narsus poured himself more wine. He'd been grateful Brightside had been the buffer and kept Cinder from bouncing into his arms when they'd walked in the door. The joyous reunions were always one-sided and made Narsus uncomfortable.

Cinder's compass swung from a chain around his neck while he flittered around the kitchen. Narsus thought his jaw would crack from having to endure the puttering. Why there were so many phoenix who were Compass-borns, he'd never know, but there were also many more who were not. It was frustrating at having his own kind around to bully him. But that had been their plan.

That wasn't the crux of what was bothering Narsus now. It was Cinder going about his chores. Narsus had worked through this. He'd been fine. Until now.

Being in Cinder's company hadn't set him off in a hundred years. He'd always cared about the Cottage phoenix, but he'd never been in love with him.

Narsus couldn't shake the sudden blanket of sorrow. He took another swallow of the fermented fruit drink before he figured it out. Cinder's excessive cheer, and especially his positive outlook, reminded him of Lune.

Narsus reached for the bottle. Brightside gave him a long, pressing look before smoothly removing it from his reach. "Face your monsters," he admonished.

Narsus lashed out. "He reeked of decaying seaweed. Or week-old fish."

"Liar," Brightside challenged sharply. "It was fresh sea spray and sun-scalded sand. Like he just washed out of the ocean. Must be Mer-born. Why are you deliberately being an asshole?"

"You know why," Cinder answered. "Because he IS an asshole. Trapped inside his own head. Verdigris isn't the only forge who has a monopoly on grief and self-destruction. But Narsus and Lune are fire and water, so it could just be Narsus trying to settle in without drowning."

Narsus rolled his eyes. Of course Cinder would know all the juicy details. Because Brightside was telepathic. The talent was so common

Narsus often forgot it existed. The elf must have been gossiping with Cinder when they came up the front walk and paused to take their shoes off. Narsus sent Brightside a round of heavy mental arrows and rocks—only to be answered with a smug smirk.

"We should do something to help our friend," Brightside said to Cinder. The elf disposed of the orange peels in a bin Cinder offered. "I recommend a coastal retreat to think about it. To the beach!"

"Yes, a wonderful idea to get him used to the water," Cinder exclaimed. "Some phoenix can be so squirmy and whiny around water."

"Oh?" Brightside said, genuinely shocked. "You do so well."

"Because of you," Cinder answered, his cheeks rosy, and his gaze caressing the elf.

Narsus crossed his arms. "Hey. I'm right here. Don't talk about me like I'm not here. If you think to try and find this Lune person—"

Brightside's attention remained on the crow-like phoenix. "We'll vacation far from a major population. Hardly anyone will be around."

"And where do you suppose we'll find room and board?" Narsus challenged, suddenly thinking that there were two-like conversations going on, but with two different meanings. "Or will you be forcing us to sleep under the stars?"

Brightside got up and selected a key from the rack of wall hooks. And finally addressed Narsus. "Your grandfather. Calico has a secluded beach house on Little Forge Island. He gave me the directions and the keys before he left for home. Unfortunately, there's only two bedrooms. So your cranky ass gets the couch in the parlor."

"If there is a couch," Cinder teased. "If not, he gets the floor and a blanket. Sounds fair. I'm off to pack."

Narsus grumbled. "Are you sure Cal's gone? I really don't want a lecture from blood relations right now. Especially my grandfather. It's bad enough I have you two harassing me."

Brightside waved the keys. "Come on, old bean. That's what Cal would say. Relax for once. Cal's treat."

Narsus sighed. "Fine. Sunbathing on a deserted stretch of sand soaking up the sun might do my mood some good. But if you both plan to sunbathe too—"

"We know, we know," Cinder said, re-appearing with stuffed satchels in hand. He handed one off to Brightside. "Twenty paces minimum distance."

"That was quick," Narsus commented dryly. "As if this was already planned ahead of time."

The two just moved to the front door and waited for him to get up. Brightside's cool and distant demeanor allowed for no refusal. Cinder just grinned, tiny orange sparks flashing around those amber-orange eyes.

Grumbling, Narsus knew he had no choice but to haul his butt out of the chair.

Waking up to discover a third jewel had burned out lured Lune into an odd mood. He snapped the compass cover shut and hurried to the docks, eager to return to his beloved Jade Raptor and the ocean.

Finding out that Sachin had taken full advantage of his absence put Lune into an additional spiral of feeling lost. Not only did his friend get the sail repaired in the day Lune had been on the trek to the temple, but his cargo hauler had scored big time. Secured a full week's work ferrying the governor of a neighboring island around on a birthday cruise. At twice the amount they'd make in a single week.

Lune was ecstatic at the marvelous luck. But he did lament the loss of a shoulder to cry on. So it was back to being a companion inside his own head and wander the beach with nothing to do.

While he did miss Calico and his stuffy ways, he reveled in not wearing clothes. Father was a stickler for manners and propriety. And especially modesty.

Fresh and dry from a relaxing, cold bath, Lune carried out his revenge by setting his bare ass on Calico's favorite chair in the parlor. He hoped he left butt-dents in the fabric.

He wiggled for good measure, settling in with a book. He'd been waiting for this text and it finally arrived in the mail. Since most folks on the island fished or raised livestock for a living, no one was too interested in the deep mechanics of vegetable gardening. The book was Cal's goodbye gift, because Lune wanted to keep growing those delicious, mouth-burning peppers with funny names that originated from another world.

But not even the printed word could distract him. There was no telling when Sachin would return. That governor was known for overstaying his welcome at parties. So waiting around for his friend to get home also meant waiting around for the innkeeper or the dock master to get back to him about a temporary job. So he could eat something that wasn't from the ocean.

As Lune tried to read, that beaked mask invaded his thoughts. What would it be like? Getting all worked up and sweaty while Narsus wore it. And what Narsus looked like underneath it. Lune shook the thoughts out of his head. No point in torturing himself.

His belly suddenly rumbled. Lune really didn't want to deal with trawling the water for his meals, but hunting while excessively hungry, could cause mistakes. Better to do it now while he had some reserve left.

With a sigh, he put down his book and pushed out of Calico's favorite chair. He grabbed the fishing spear out of the closet. It would be nice to wallow under the waves for a while and get Narsus—Mr. Attitude out of his head.

Lune paused at the water's edge, looking out across the serene glimmers. It suddenly struck him how lonely he was. But not lonely enough to subject himself to someone who didn't, or wouldn't even try to be interested in him.

Wading into the waves, Lune let the current guide him out to his next meal.

Chapter 7

GRANDFATHER'S BEACH HOUSE WAS bright, clean, and larger than Narsus expected. It was surprisingly cozy and modern. Whitewashed shiplap planks made up the walls and A-framed ceiling.

The family room hosted fluffy area rugs and three sturdy chairs arranged around a low table. A lit candelabra hung from above, as if they'd been expected. Magic, probably. Set off when they walked in.

Cinder breezed into the room with an armload of blankets. "Bree picked the open ocean-side room," he reported. "So that means I get the master with the cozy fireplace. Here are your blankets for the couch."

Narsus took another hurried look around. "There's no couch. You'll be sleeping in the fireplace, like always, so Bree can take the bed in your room. I'll take his."

"No." Cinder crossed his arms. "Not happening. The bed in the master suite faces the window. That view's too lovely to give up. Besides, I'm not sharing a room with you. So you're sleeping out here on the floor. Or you're welcome to try and sleep in a chair."

Narsus took a closer look at one of the chairs. What he saw made him cringe.

"What? Why do you have that look on your face?"

Narsus pointed to said chair while looking around, half-expecting a stranger to emerge from somewhere else in the house.

Leaning over to look, Cinder sent him a glance askance. "Why are you showing me Calico's naked butt-indents? The fabric pattern is lovely, though."

"That's not Calico's bare ass indents. My grandfather wouldn't be caught dead naked. They obviously belong to someone else."

Cinder's carefree shrugs annoyed him. "I won't tell Calico about the ball-sweat chair if you don't."

Narsus closed his eyes and counted to three. "We'll have it cleaned—the house professionally cleaned before we leave. Or else he'll blame it on one of us and I'll never hear the end of it."

Long swims usually cleared the cobwebs from Lune's mind. But he always felt dizzy and nauseous if he tried to venture beyond the depths of a ten minute dive. Heading back toward the surface always eased the pressure. So he often spent his days loitering around the reef. Water predators usually left him alone now that he was full grown. *Guh. Water predators. Sharks.* Time to get dry land under his toes.

The few fish Lune had collected would help supplement and stretch his week's allowance. It would have to do. Despite Calico going out of his way to fix elaborate sea-fare spreads, just for him, Lune hated seafood. He'd rather eat what Calico ate. Sugary desserts. Lots of fruits and vegetables with the occasional pork and beef.

Hitting the beach was always like a blast of air directly into his face. More so now that he coughed up the water that had slipped into his lungs. His skin tingled as it began to dry out and his gills sealed shut against his neck. It always took a second to get his equilibrium back.

Tilting his head and tapping the water out of his ears, he stopped in his tracks. The waves lapping against the shore curled around his ankles and rhythmically pounded against his butt.

It was as if the waves mimicked his thoughts when Lune locked eyes with the most gorgeous hunk of male he'd ever seen. Correction: A very fit and naked male. Who lounged on a beach towel completely without clothing. Did Lune say the man was sans clothing?

Why was there a naked man on Calico's beach?

Er, his beach now.

While Lune was working up the courage to say hello, another thought crossed his mind. What if Calico had come back? With husband Agustin in tow?

No, Calico would've called out to him the instant he emerged from the water. Or sent out a telepathic greeting when he and said party arrived. His father would not lounge around naked, or permit others to do so.

Lune glanced further up the beach. There were two others with this stranger, but to Lune, they blurred and merged with the sandy beach. Because he only had eyes for the one closest to him.

Wait. No. These were trespassers. On his beach. On his property. But Lune was too busy soaking up the vision before him.

The naked man had shiny and dark iridescent green feathers scattered around his body. There was a nest of those gleaming feathers at his nether regions. Lune blinked, immediately lifting his gaze from the rather impressive...*snake*...that rested there.

Lune felt the blush rising in his cheeks. Great gods, what was wrong with him that he couldn't even think the proper word without getting flustered? He'd absorbed too much of Calico's fussy and modest lifestyle.

It was at that moment Lune realized he, too, was naked. He forced himself not to shield his privates. What must he look like slogging out of the surf like some exhausted sea monster beaching himself to die? He knew he shouldn't have stayed under so long, but it was half self-punishment and half-testing the depths he could go. Really, the only thing that had expelled him from his swim was the pressure of the ocean, and the shark flashback.

His excitement over this mysterious stranger suddenly made his stomach sink. Because the compass he'd secured around his wrist began to glow.

Oh, by the goddess, *really?* This was the jerk who couldn't even be bothered to come to the altar? Now he was trespassing!

Lune had to act cool. Aloof. Turn the tables. Act as disinterested and annoyed as Narsus had when they first met. And maybe even gross him out. So Lune advanced with purpose. Locking eyes with Narsus, he slowly took a big bite out of the dead fish impaled on his spear.

The scales and raw flesh mulched around in his mouth, and Lune tried to ignore the slimy sensation. Chewing slowly, he was gagging inside and hoped it wasn't showing on his face. Despite being a siren, having raw fish and scales stuck between his teeth was even more disgusting than the baked fish Calico often prepared. But he'd be damned if his escaped groom could lounge on his property looking all attractive with slim muscles all glistening in the sun.

Narsus held his breath and nearly splashed himself with his iced tea. His Compass-husband rose from the ocean like a god. A fierce and displeased ocean god. Naked as the day of his birth.

Narsus knew it was Lune. Felt it not just deep in his bones, but in his heart. He was glad he was sitting down, thus covering up the glowing, tingly Compass-mark on his ass cheek.

Lune's straw-colored hair molded against his cheeks and shoulders, highlighting the planes and angles of his heart-shaped face. Showcasing the deep, glittering, rich ambers and browns of his candidly angry and fiery eyes. His Intended's flat belly was rock hard. Chiseled. As if he worked those stomach muscles for hours each day. Perhaps he had, as it seemed the ocean was intimate to him.

Narsus dropped his gaze lower. There was no shrinkage from the cool waters. Which meant he did have some sort of Mer in his blood. There was also a bit of rise in that dick as they stared at each other.

Lune huffed at him. A signal he'd been caught staring. Narsus lifted his eyes to encounter disdain and irritation. Embarrassment heated Narsus's face. He deserved that. Brightside and Cinder were right. He'd reacted harshly. Because he'd been afraid of hurting his Compass-mate. Still not yet ready to trust himself with his own poisonous abilities, despite centuries of practice.

Too wrapped up inside his own fears.

Fears that included this being yet another Compass-glitch.

And mostly, he didn't know if he could deal with being hurt again.

This meeting, this second chance... Was it truly a sign that Lune was his fated mate? Was this the magic of the compass—Lune's compass—drawing them back together?

It would've been easier if Lune was a phoenix—but even then there'd be a repeat of his original contemplations—and the same questions about his poisons and their physical compatibility.

Maybe it *was* time to try and make amends. To see if this was a true, genuine Compass-match after all. Was he strong enough to take the chance?

·♥·♥·♥·♥·♥·

Lune wouldn't have any of this nonsense. Why, how was this jerk even here? On *HIS* beach, lounging in front of *HIS* house? Perhaps the compass had led the way here—if Narsus even had it to begin with.

Maybe the jerk was sorry and wanted to make amends. As soon as that crossed his mind, Lune scoffed inwardly. Laying naked on a beach wasn't the way to apologize, and it certainly didn't appear that was what his Intended wanted to do. In fact, Narsus's behavior was taunting and haughty.

It was a surprise to view him in the altogether. He wasn't as scary and intimidating without his mask, hat, and cape. In fact, Lune was getting the impression of someone defiantly vulnerable. If that was such a thing.

Lune suddenly snapped himself out of the sympathetic lure. So what if those thick, flat eyebrows framed those wary, dark green eyes in shadows. That piercing gaze still cut through him with disdain and judgment. Although, it was softened by the windswept green hair hiding round ears that stuck out slightly.

Those sharp features stood out and faintly glowed on a very pale, but not quite sickly complexion. The square jaw highlighting those hallowed, clean-shaven cheekbones made Lune think of the undead. Especially paired with the thinness of his form. But he couldn't be sure. Especially since Narsus was airing everything out and distracting him.

Lune knew he couldn't show weakness. So feigning indifference, and with his stomach muscles clenching, he brought the speared fish back to his mouth. He forced another bite and chewed, staring his Compass-husband in the eyes. And radiating the full dare me energy that was rushing through his veins.

The sound of a book suddenly slammed shut and that elf—Brightside gasped. "Lune? That *is* you."

"Oh, by the gods, this *is* fate!" The bubbly cry and energy came from another phoenix-in-human-form who sat next to Brightside. Little orange flames framed his face at the hairline. When the phoenix ran his hands through his curls, the flames elongated from the downward pressure, then sprang back into tiny embers. "Narsus, he's adorable! Hello Lune, my name is Cinder, of the Cottage phoenix forge. I'm Bree's housekeeper."

"We're all friends," Brightside corrected, watching a stoic Narsus. "Although Cinder is fairly obsessed with a domestic role. Lune, so I take it this means you're a local to this island?"

"I am." Lune strove for calm and neutrality. "You're actually all loitering on my property, and apparently, in my house."

"This is my grandfather's property," Narsus claimed flatly while reaching for his hat and cloak.

Grandfather? "I grew up here," Lune snapped back. It was one thing to act aloof, but now his home was being threatened. "This beach house and the beach front is mine now. Calico filed the deed several days ago."

Brightside's brows shot up. "You know Calico?"

"Calico's my foster father," Lune clarified with pride, his glare pinned on Narsus. "He raised me from a stray egg that washed ashore. Would you mind getting your big feet out of my nursery tide pool?"

Narsus stared him down as he slowly complied.

"The sun's setting," Cinder cut in. "Why don't we all head inside and talk about this over hot tea and think about dinner? Oh, um," he hurried. "With your permission, Lune?"

Lune considered a course of action. "There's no food in the house. Calico gave it all away to the townsfolk before I left for the marriage temple." Narsus avoided his returned stare at that point. "Calico's not here. He retired. To the world his husband lives in, apparently."

"That's unfortunate we missed him." Brightside shook the sand off his beach towel. "We'll have to go into town for a meal, then. Narsus's treat. Please do join us, Lune. We'll do the marketing in the morning."

"In the morning? No, no thank you for the dinner invite. No, you can't stay here," Lune protested.

"But it's late," Narsus cut in.

"I'm aware of the day and night cycles," Lune bit back, then realized just how late it really was. His jaw tightened as he remembered his manners. *Thanks, Cal,* he thought with sarcasm. *Thanks loads for giving me a conscience.* Cal would never turn someone out, and would be very disappointed in him if he did so. But then Cal was smart enough to never be in the position to have to accommodate guests. Invited or uninvited.

"Yes, I know it's late," Lune said. "The inns are closed, and you missed the last boat off the island. Fine. You can all stay. But just for tonight."

It was at this time Lune remembered he'd been standing here, exposed. Without another word, he just hurried into the house and made a beeline into the master bedroom. He eyed the rucksack on the bed and frowned as he buttoned up a pair of trousers. As soon as he'd done that, there was a timid knock at the door.

It was Cinder. "I apologize. I had no idea this was your room. I'll bunk with Bree. May I retrieve my bag?"

Lune stepped aside and Cinder hurriedly claimed it. The thought of where Narsus was going to sleep shouldn't concern him. He was asking before he could stop himself. "If you and Brightside are in the second bedroom—"

"Oh, we already decided he's got the 'couch'." Cinder chuckled and left with a wink.

Lune grinned. Maybe sleeping on the cold tile floor would give his Compass-husband an attitude adjustment.

Chapter 8

BEING THE LAST ONE to enter, and leave the outside bath house, Narsus showered the sand out of his cracks and folds. Then used the hose to spray down the area, just in case any oils from his body lingered.

He sat stiffly in the beach house parlor—fully dressed and fiddling with the sculpted leather of his father's beaked mask. It was a little unnerving to have so many people around him in such a confined, unfamiliar space. He took a deep breath, then bent his head to exhale into the thick scarf he kept around his neck. When he got nervous, he sometimes exhaled a miasma of toxic fumes.

Cinder had made more tea, and now extended a glass to him. Narsus hesitated, and sent Brightside a subtle glance. Only when the elf silently encouraged him with a beaming gaze above his cup did he accept it. Narsus knew he had to get over the trauma of simple interaction with Cinder—but this forced proximity with both Cinder *and* Lune was making him a wreck. Narsus controlled his shaking hands by using both of them to steady the glass.

It was Lune who broke the tense silence. "If you're more comfortable with your companions here, for what I have to say to you, that's fine. But if you'd rather do this in private, that's fine too."

It was difficult to start with everyone staring at him, but he'd done this to himself. It was time to try and explain his behavior. Narsus motioned for his friends to leave. Not making a fool of himself in front of Brightside and Cinder was ideal. And, he'd rather not have Cinder around right now making him even more uncomfortable.

"We'll see if we can get some food somewhere." Brightside pulled on a loitering Cinder, who was grinning, obviously wanting his ear to the juicy drama.

As they exited, Lune called out, "There's a farmhouse about a mile up the road. Tell them I sent you."

They nodded and left.

"I wanted to apologize," Narsus began, fingers tapping on his mask. "This isn't easy for me."

"Because you're a Verdigris," Lune finished for him. "A phoenix full of poison. Born of a phoenix forge who cannot touch."

Narsus blinked. "How did you know? There aren't that many Verdi-grises here in the Star Land archipelago."

There was a half-smile. "This is the farthest island from the main island, but we're not *that* isolated out here. Our schools are top-notch, run by Elders who hire retired teachers from the main island. It was pretty easy to confirm what you were when I saw you on the beach just now. And, it kind of helped me understand why you're an asshole."

Narsus cracked a reluctant grin. "I figure you had other phoenix as teachers, besides my grandfather?"

Lune laughed. "That phoenix teacher you speak of was Calico himself. See? We're getting along. Talking civilly. I don't understand why you didn't give us a chance."

Narsus turned his head away. The breath in his lungs momentarily escaping in his nervousness. "My poison. I'm toxic to the touch."

Lune leaned forward. "Even if you don't believe in the compass, I do. What more proof do you want? Your grandfather raised me! How marvelous is that? May I tell you a bit about myself?"

It took a moment of gathering his courage for Narsus to nod.

"I'm not human. I'm of siren heritage even though I've never been able to shift. But I never tried, really," he added. "Bipedalism suits me too well—even though I breathe underwater just fine. I can stay down indefinitely. In fact, I kind of prefer the water and don't like being on land much. I do act a bit drunk and disoriented when I first surface though, if I've been down for hours. I have to get used to dry land again."

Narsus tried not to feel endearment. Getting to know more about Lune was making it harder to keep his distance. He had to keep his distance. For their own good.

Lune kept talking. "I don't know if I'm a half-breed or not, but I've been stung by jellyfish. Bit by certain poison octopi—the one with blue rings. I've never gotten sick. Or died, obviously."

Lune talking about dying was a prickly subject to a phoenix—even an undead one, so Narsus ignored the mention. Compass-mate or not, if you weren't phoenix-born, you would never know a phoenix's secrets. The sanity and life of their race depended on it.

Narsus frowned as the rest of the story filtered into his brain. "Those are sea creatures you mention. I'm undead. Of fire and air. Another reason you and I are incompatible."

"Maybe we should test that sometime." Lune's hand reached out, palm up. "We are Compass-matched after all."

"I don't think so." Narsus hid quivering hands before they became fists. He didn't want to commit to something so dangerous. He couldn't bear for someone to be hurt. Or suffer. Again. Because of him. Was Lune a thrill-seeker, or just didn't care about his own life?

Lune brought his compass into view, as if to prove his words as truth. "We can't be that incompatible, or do you not believe in the magic?"

Being questioned on this belief made him uncomfortable. Because he had lost faith. He also didn't want to explain his personal, tragic details. "My heritages are visible. Something I can see and know to be the truth."

"When did you meet other Compass-bearers? They seem very comfortable with you."

Lune changing the subject was suspicious. Maybe he could read body language. Maybe the siren understood this line of questioning was getting too much for him to handle. But that was impossible, especially since his Intended had been raised by Calico, the master of adorable bumbling cluelessness.

"Brightside and Cinder have been my friends for ages."

"Where are their Compass-mates?"

"They don't have one. Not as yet. We were housemates for a few centuries. Before I figured it was better to—uh, safer to live on my own." That was, of course, when Cinder 'died.'

"So you don't see their hope for success either?"

Narsus skirted the question. "The three of us each have our own troubles."

Lune was leaning forward, staring holes into him. "What troubles? Or is it too personal to share?"

Why was he squirming in his chair like a five-year-old in trouble? "We've all been waiting a few centuries for our calls. Most other Compass-bearers are paired and living happily ever after before their quarter century mark."

Lune was staring at him funny. Narsus suddenly wondered if what he'd just said had been voiced too sarcastically.

Lune seemed to accept his answer, but posed one of his own. "Those paired—were they elves and phoenix too?"

Narsus took that minute to think. "I'm not exactly sure, but a handful of them were definitely human. Other races too."

"There you go, then." Lune gave a smart nod, as if that explained everything. "Elves and phoenix are long-lived beings. Humans aren't. It makes perfect sense if the magic paired humans off so quickly."

"There's no proof of that," Narsus scoffed. "Of your theory, I mean."

Lune pressed the glass of iced tea against his neck. "You would know, being the one educated in Compass-lore. Being a god and all."

"I'm...I'm not a god."

Lune shrugged. "Demi-god, then."

There wasn't any sense in arguing it. Especially since Lune didn't seem to treat him with any divine favor. More likely, interacting with deities held no mystery for this siren, as he'd been raised by Cal. So Lune had most certainly associated with extended family during family gatherings and festivals—activities which he himself always avoided.

Lune was still dabbing the glass of iced tea against his sweaty neck. Narsus tried not to watch, fascinated at the gentle undulation of those gills. He was horrified at the urge to lick them. Then trail down lower to score a possessive bite.

A bite? What had prompted that urge? He barely ever got blood-urges.

Narsus gripped the armchair rest. What in Nolth's flying death barge was happening? The fangs he'd done his best to keep hidden suddenly felt so very heavy. So very empty. With a slight, aching pang that wasn't to be ignored. He thought he'd been safe. Because he'd never had the urge or desire for blood. Or consider the heady tang of an ocean-blood. Would Lune taste of salty brine? Or of the ocean breeze?

Lune wiped the sweat off his upper lip.

Sweat. A salty-delicious dampness that was the prelude to a glorious meal. With just a taste, Narsus knew he'd be well satiated.

No. Stop it.

Back to the sweat. Narsus tried to convince himself it was more proof they weren't a true pairing. Lune couldn't take the heat of the tropical Star Lands. The fire goddess—his great-grandmother—created the Star Lands archipelago eons ago, specifically for a phoenix's comfort.

Narsus sighed. Trying to get Lune to accept that his Compass-lore theories were wrong wasn't working. When he didn't keep the conversation going, Lune veered in yet another direction.

After another sip of tea, Lune said, "The priests wanted me to come back for an orientation on Compass-lore, but I declined. I was getting antsy being away from my cove."

"The compass never summoned you for an orientation?" Narsus asked in true surprise. "Everyone who's Compass-born has been through orientation when they come of age." Narsus was puzzled at the furrowed brows and uncertain frown on Lune's face.

"N-no. When was that supposed to have happened?"

"When the compass first manifests." Narsus wanted to prove his point, but didn't want to appear disagreeable. Instead, he bit his cheek, checking the placement of his fangs with his tongue. The longer he sat here, the longer the urge to take a nip manifested.

Oh Nolth, not again. He wasn't lisping around his fangs like a god-damn fledgling-biter, was he? He was too old for this. Even more annoying was the term of fledgling. It was used by phoenix as well. He felt mocked and tormented over this second double entendre.

"Compass-magic does glitch from time to time, as it was—still is technically, an experimental magic."

"Oh," Lune said, looking inward. "That I didn't know. Is that why you're reluctant?"

Narsus tried to catch his breath and conceal the anxiety and grief rising within him. And at this strange, sudden thirst. He wanted to keep his shame and sorrow hidden. But if Lune spent any more time with Brightside, the truth would slip out, eventually. Not that Brightside would gossip. The elf was a trusted friend. It would just be Lune asking innocent questions that Brightside would avoid. And that would raise Lune's suspicions.

Thoughts of Brightside reminded him to try and live. His dear friend had carried him through so much trauma after Cinder's demise. The least he could do to repay that love and kindness was to try.

Live! He could still hear the elf scream and plead with him after Cinder died. *Narsus! Fight, damn you. Fight!*

"I..." His throat dried up. He tried again. "I..."

"Take as long as you want," Lune said softly.

Why had he started to say anything? This was stupid. Without realizing, he slipped his beaked mask over his face. His eyes were tearing, and he didn't want to feel vulnerable. Not in front of Lune. Not right now. He was so raw. But the sudden memory of Cinder's—the old Cinder's—last smile of love and forgiveness, for him, opened the scars criss-crossing his heart.

"I...hurt someone I thought was my match," Narsus finally said. "We both thought we were a match. In the end, he...suffered and died from my poison. *My touch.* Even Verdigris Healers summoned from the mainland of Nura couldn't reverse the damage."

He could never, ever, reveal Cinder's identity. Even though phoenix were known to be reborn, the exact measure of those hows, whys, and whens were race-secrets. Lest someone discover it and use it against them for harmful and degrading purposes. It was bad enough Brightside was aware there had been a rebirth.

It was a moment before Lune spoke. "Narsus, I'm so sorry."

He flinched when Lune reached out to comfort. The hand slowly rescinded.

Narsus so wanted to tell Lune that his mistaken-chosen had been a phoenix. That they had been reborn and now thrived without him. But the pain and suffering he and Cinder endured wasn't to be taken lightly. Both of them had grieved and been traumatized by the ordeal. His false mate had to have his memory purged by the united phoenix forges to save his sanity. All memories of the ordeal, and of Narsus himself being his Compass-mate, had been erased.

Narsus couldn't help but glance toward the door, glad that Cinder had recovered. Glad that Brightside had been there for Cinder when he himself could never be.

"Narsus?" Lune's voice was soft. "Would you rather take a break? I can brew more tea."

A break from the subject would be eagerly embraced, but not from the company. That was yet another surprise of the night. He desperately wanted Lune to stay. To sit here and be with him.

But his thirst. His fangs. His poison. Why was he torturing himself?

Maybe he'd taken on too much to accept and deal with all at once. Maybe he hadn't been fair to himself while trying to be fair to Lune. Afraid to answer, Narsus got up without a word and walked out. Before he opened his mouth and repeated another "You'll do," mistake.

And wanting to assuage his need—this prickly urge—to feed from the emergency blood pills the Grim always insisted he carry.

Alone.

A plated ham sandwich materialized into Narsus's view, knocking him out of his heavy thoughts. Even though it was well into the night, the magical crystal lenses of his beaked mask and the light of the moon clearly defined the one who held it.

Narsus had been focused intently on the roar of the surf and the twinkling of the stars while mired in what was. Trying to quell the chaos of his mind among the familiar isolation of just sitting in the sand.

Lune stood over him, but again, not too close. Looped over Lune's other arm was the roped handle of a small metal bucket. The bucket was rusted with age from saltwater and time. The faded paint flaking off it revealed the childishly crude artwork of two fat birds—one white, and one green. Between them was a smiling, blond-haired, two-tailed Mer. The handle of a little shovel rose above the bucket's rim.

The white bird—was obviously Calico. The Mer had to be Lune's self-portrait. And the green one? Narsus nibbled on his lip as he pondered, wondering if it was a depiction of him, via the premonition magic of the compass.

"Your friends got back with some supplies. I thought you'd be hungry." Lune's voice broke into his thoughts.

He was hungry for solid food, but he'd never admit to it. "Thank you." Narsus accepted the plate and stared at it. Toasted slices of thick sourdough contained lettuce and tomato. Among it was a healthy chunk of ham. His stomach growled, causing him to push the beaked mask up to rest on his forehead.

Lune was feeding him. Such a simple offering chipped away at his defenses. It was a silly and amusing revelation. Narsus took a bite, letting the fresh flavors and delicious crunch of lettuce and toasted bread overtake his tastebuds.

Setting to work, Lune used the bucket to scoop out a good six inches of sand. He discarded the catch, retrieved water from the surf, then secured the bucket snugly in the well. The rim sat even with the surrounding sand.

Narsus watched with curiosity as he ate. "What are you doing?"

"I thought I'd keep you company." Lune's fingers flit about in the sand. "Dabble in some art while we chat. If that's okay with you."

That cheerful smile made the pit of Narsus's belly feel funny. Turned his insides, out. The sensations distressed him, and he clamped his fangs in his mouth as a precaution. Grateful that the pills he hardly ever consumed, until now, quelled the blood hunger.

"I—I guess it's fine. Sure." Narsus checked the state of his fangs with his tongue. Then took another bite of his sandwich, letting the tang of sauces and salt and pepper take hold. "What are you making?"

"Oh, this is just a drawing."

Narsus clenched his jaw as the image took further shape. The curved lines and strokes created a compass. Right down to the jewels. Lune used the natural tools at hand for the details: stray twigs, pebbles, even bits of seaweed.

Narsus couldn't be mad. He was actually quite impressed at Lune sneaking the subject into their interaction. "You're obviously talented."

"Thanks." Lune's focus fractured, and he glanced over. "You're looking at the sand-art champion of Little Forge Island eight years in a row. However, I did lose this year's competition."

Narsus wondered why humor attacked the corner of his mouth, causing it to turn up. "Who bested such an experienced king?"

Lune's bark of laughter hit him with a wave of joyous energy. It penetrated Narsus's bones and lingered with jubilant wisps of warmth.

"A class of school children," Lune said. "They combined their talents and prided themselves on teamwork. At their award speech, they declared their intent to hold onto their new title. Then they all turned and stared at me."

Narsus chuckled. "And your response to that pressure?"

"I wisely retired. Publicly. On the spot."

That made Narsus laugh aloud.

"I had my reign, and my fun." Lune looked up from his work again and smiled. "It was time to pass on the crown. Especially since they said I'd been their inspiration. Thinking back over the years, I recall some of them tailing the judges and furiously taking notes."

"That *is* dedication," Narsus agreed.

Lune candidly smothered his mirth. "Or intimidation tactics."

Narsus paused a moment. "I have a difficult time picturing you intimidated. You're too sunny a personality."

"I strive to find the positive in my experiences. Although I don't always succeed."

Lune stared him directly in the eyes, then. Narsus winced and lowered his gaze. Guilt prickled. He turned his attention toward the sand art to escape.

What he saw there only intensified the scrutiny he felt himself avoiding. Lune's depiction of the compass fixated on the jeweled countdown. The long stick in the siren's hand tapped at the current jewel that had gone dark, as if posing the question. Giving him a chance to explain. It was an inquiry Narsus wouldn't answer. So he ignored it instead.

The few moments of silence had Lune attacking him from a different angle. "What makes us special?" Lune's stick withdrew from toying with the pebbles representing the jewels. He surrendered it to the sand. "To be chosen."

Here it was. The uncomfortable exploration into their Compass-match. "Nothing. The magic is randomly sewn into our souls."

"So it's not something passed down?"

Narsus shrugged. "It can be, but it's rare. Compass-individuals are born with a jewel seed inside them. When they're born, it remains within them, manifesting upon their palm, on their chest, or where ever. The placement of my birthmark just happens to match yours—a similar design—on our ass cheeks. That's not always true for each couple. When Compass-borns are coherent enough, their compass manifests on the physical plane."

Lune nodded. "The morning of my twelfth birthday. I awoke with a compass in my grip."

Narsus gave a quick glance. "Interesting. That's one of the youngest ages I've ever heard of."

"Really?"

Narsus shrugged, trying to cover how surprised he'd been. "Average age is about fifteen. I was a late-bloomer at nineteen and a half. But Compass-magic is often thought of as somewhat sentient. It won't manifest if the bearer isn't in the correct mindset, or mired in an unstable environment. Often, in times of distress, the compass might revert back inside the body, or not manifest at all."

Lune slowly picked up the stick again and traced a curve in the sand already created. "So one could say you're still not in the correct mindset? But you had your compass and now it's not here—I haven't seen it about your person. So it makes me wonder if you still don't know what you want yourself."

It took all Narsus had not to snap out in defense. Lune knew nothing about him and had the nerve to judge. He pulled down his mask and folded his arms. "Thank you for your hospitality. We'll be gone in the morning."

A few seconds ticked by before Lune stood and brushed himself off. It was easy to sense when he walked away. Part of Narsus felt the emptiness where the warmth of his presence had previously been. Oddly, the absence hurt more now than it ever had in the past. Gripping his elbows, he looked out through the crystal lenses of his mask. And forced his attention to remain fixed upon the rhythmic calmness of the ocean.

Chapter 9

Lune woke up to the clap of thunder. Seconds later, torrential rain pounded on the roof of the little beach house. Snuggling back down into his own covers, Lune was startled even further when he heard the sliding glass door bump shut. He sat up. He'd forgotten all about his guests as soon as his head touched the pillow. He'd been so exhausted over the last few days, and yesterday had been a doozy.

He knew his old room was secure, having heard the slider-wall close earlier in the evening. Brightside and Cinder should be fine, as there were also extra blankets in the closet should they need them.

In the parlor, if the slider door was open, of course rain gave the room a good soaking. The furniture was made to take a beating from the wet weather, but there'd be a new lake across the tile floor. Where Narsus slept.

Why should he be worried about the phoenix jerk who was out there with two little blankets that were now probably drenched from the storm?

Gritting his teeth, Lune flipped back the covers. Why should he be feeling sorry for someone who'd been dismissive, abrupt, and rude? Someone who didn't even care about his feelings? Lune felt the apology had been valid, but also sensed Narsus was holding back.

Throwing on a robe, Lune padded out of his suite. A glance down the hallway showed the door to his childhood room remained shut. He could pick out the faint snores from one of the men.

The quiet grumbling from the parlor had Lune creeping forward. Peeking out from the hallway entrance, he watched Narsus peel off soaked clothing and try to dry his long hair with a kitchen tea towel.

Before Lune could stop himself, he pulled two thick bath towels from the hallway washroom's linen closet. On second thought, he collected a robe and other items. Then marched right into the waterlogged parlor.

Startled at the rapid, unannounced entry, Narsus grasped at his cloak, pulling it against his body. Lune was splashing forward. Without a shred of caution. At that rate of speed, they'd likely collide. Automatically, he tried to make himself smaller, to take up less space.

Narsus wasn't sure if it was to hide his naked body, or to keep Lune from coming into skin-to-skin contact. Maybe it was both. But the former thought was a silly one, as Lune already knew what he looked like. Right down to his dick. And already knew not to crowd him. For both their safety.

"STAY BACK!" Narsus immediately covered his mouth as soon as his gums itched and his teeth clacked. His fangs had appeared in all their glory. There'd even been an embarrassing warning hiss.

"There's no need to shout." Lune winced, dumping dry linens on the end table against the far wall. "Even I know sleeping in soaking wet clothes, in a puddle of water, isn't good for a phoenix. Come see me, first door on the right if you want somewhere warm and dry to sleep."

His Intended made a quick, smooth loop and returned to the hallway.

·♥·♥·♥·♥·♥·

Lune sank against his bedroom door once he closed it.

Oh, dear gods. Those fangs! Bright white and flashing as Narsus shouted at him. But the clamor didn't fill him with fear or dread. He knew Narsus wouldn't hurt him. If his Intended wanted, he could've already done so, out here where it was so isolated no one would find a body for weeks. Land and oceanic scavengers as well as the humidity would take care of the rest.

But what had he been thinking! Inviting a stranger to come sleep in his personal private bed? Even if that stranger was his fated Compass-mate. Lune sighed. Couples usually got to know each other *before* committing to their sacred union of a single bed. A marriage bed.

It was no use. The poisonous oils of Narsus's skin and phoenix feathers would never let Narsus take the chance, even if he himself was willing. Because Lune believed in the compass and the magic, even if Narsus did not.

Dejected, Lune didn't even bother to shed his night robe. But just flopped face first into his pillow. Embarrassed he'd made Narsus feel threatened enough to bellow at him. With those fangs. Fangs that gave him little, shivering hot flashes. Of lust. Lust? Really?

Lune was equally embarrassed he'd come off as offended and prickly. He tried to tell himself they'd both been startled, with Narsus being the more vulnerable party.

Those fangs, though... What would it feel like to have them glide across his skin? As a gentle nibble. A nudge? In a warm, laughing smile pressed into the crook of his neck? Lune twitched in surprise. A smile coming from Narsus felt like a foreign concept, but it was one that invaded his thoughts and lingered.

Lune grabbed his pillow and shoved it over his head as a distraction. The only thing soothing him back to sleep was the damp hem of his robe and his wet feet.

·♥·♥·♥·♥·♥·

When the bedroom door clicked shut and echoed from the hall, Narsus eagerly reached for the dry towels. Among them was a robe, socks, and gloves that surely belonged to Calico. Narsus held those gloves to his heart. Items he didn't even have to ask for.

Lune had come to his rescue without him having to ask. Or grovel. First impressions mattered, and Narsus knew he'd failed miserably, time and again. Head bowed, he indeed knew himself an asshole.

What to do? He really didn't want to sleep in a room with an inch of rain on the cold tile floor. That would make a phoenix seriously ill—even an undead one. So he could either throw a tantrum and sit here and be miserable, or he could take the scary step and admit Lune was right. In doing so, he had to be an adult and go knock on the door as instructed.

Acting like the adult he was, was...exhausting. Bracing himself, he dug through his pack for more blood pills. He swallowed another handful of the delicate gelatin capsules. Shivering in excitement as one popped on impact. A quick glass of water rinsed his teeth clean of any residue.

Then he pulled himself through the hallway. But he was having trouble lifting his hand to knock for entry. Gritting his teeth, he squeezed his eyes shut and put a single knuckle to the polished door. The sound was soft. To his mind and ears though, it was a pounding force, and he cringed.

When the door opened, he was more surprised than anything. He really hadn't expected entry, even at the previous invite. He'd tried to convince himself it was just a polite formality. That it didn't mean he should accept.

Lune stood there, looking all drowsy and sweetly rumpled, robe nearly hanging off one shoulder. Narsus was grateful there were no I told you so's, or visible gloating. Just Lune stepping aside.

Narsus stifled the urge to tell him to cover up for his own safety. Lune was an adult. He'd welcomed literal poison into his room, and knew how dangerous physical contact would be.

Lune grunted. "I'm about to fall on my face I'm so exhausted."

He looked it. While Lune might sleep tonight, Narsus knew he certainly wouldn't get any. He was too afraid of hurting this person who obviously had more faith and trust in him than he did himself.

"Come to bed." Lune motioned to said contraption.

Narsus stood ramrod straight. "Bed? This one bed? Where's the other?"

Lune made a sleepy noise that sounded a lot like mocking. "There is no other bed, because Cal's never had guests stay over. Doesn't matter, anyway. We're married. My bed is your bed. It's late and I'm super grumpy. Get your perky little ass in the bed."

Heat seared across Narsus's face. "Perky...? Ah, uh, this bed. Is it your personal private bed?"

Narsus white-knuckled the closure of his robe. Was he ready for this step? Personal private beds were only for general family bonding. Or cementing the intimate commitment of wedlock. Or for marital pleasure. Or to make babies with your chosen life-mate.

Lune rolled his eyes and made a rude noise. "Yes. We're married," he repeated. "It's fine."

"But—"

Lune rounded on him. "I'm sure Brightside and Cinder are squeezed onto the one in my old room. And yes, there's only one bed in there, too."

"That's different," Narsus defended. "Bree and Cinder are family found. And besides, that isn't their personal private bed, anyway."

Rolling his eyes skyward, again, Lune sighed. "Dear gods, you are sooo related to Calico. Proper and stuffy to the core. I wonder if this stupid custom is followed outside the Star Land Islands."

"It is," Narsus clarified.

Narsus knew this was ridiculous. His fears were ridiculous. Technically, Lune was right. They *were* married. Narsus pursed his lips, wondering what he was really worried about more. Proper custom or his poison soaking into the sheets? Both maybe? Or was he just too nervous, and he was trying to find flimsy excuses? Wrapping himself in a blanket should do. He also had dry gloves and socks to safeguard against any transmission.

Coming over, he saw the bed was indeed large enough. A quality mattress that didn't sag in the middle. They wouldn't be rolling into each other, at least. Narsus hoped his relief didn't show. He would crowd himself upon the edge, rigidly locked and shrunk in on himself. But he was even more surprised when Lune opened the closet and brought out a long, narrow foot board.

"What is that?" Narsus asked. It wasn't wide enough to sleep atop of.

"A bundling board."

"A what?"

Lune didn't answer, but neatly slid the plank into slots on the head board and foot board. Then threw him a pile of his own blankets. "A compromise. If it will make you less stressed out, you have your side, and I'll have mine."

Narsus couldn't make up his mind if he should be relieved or insulted. In the end, though, it was a relief. He was too tired to inquire of its existence. He might catch a few winks tonight after all.

Following Lune's lead, he climbed in, fully clothed. Or at least as fully clothed as the robe, gloves, and socks Lune provided him. He started braiding his hair lest the strands fling over the board and onto Lune's face if he tossed and turned.

"This is just for tonight, you understand." Lune snuffed out the bedside lamp. "You'll leave in the morning and find other accommodations."

"We'll likely just head back," Narsus found himself answering. Then, after a few minutes. "I apologize, again. I didn't know this was your home."

There was a harrumph. "Meaning you wouldn't have come if you'd known?"

He'd walked right into that one. Narsus thought the question semi-hostile and reined in his own barbed response. It wasn't either of their fault for being Compass-born. "Meaning that I would have asked before we entered." There, that sounded neutral enough.

"So you were coming to find me after all?"

There was a shred of hope in response. Narsus wanted to kick himself. He was just digging himself in deeper. He wouldn't voice it, but no. He wouldn't have come. At the time, he would have just ignored and tried to forget.

What could he say without being too hurtful? "Meaning that I didn't know you were Calico's fosterling, or that this was your home."

"Oh."

Narsus felt Lune's crestfallen disappointment in his gut. The guilt was creeping further along. Why couldn't they just go to sleep? Wasn't Lune exhausted?

"Do you intend to submit a divorce?"

Did Lune even know what he was asking? The idea of a divorce hadn't even crossed Narsus's mind, given that earlier he hadn't even cared about the marriage itself. Because the embedded gems counting down would take care of that if the compasses weren't tapped together.

And after the compasses were clicked together, there was no such thing as a divorce. Despite any rare magical glitches, the matches were too precise, and to cleave the two from the bond-magic itself meant emotional trauma for the rest of their days.

"No," Narsus said immediately. "No divorce." And surprised himself that he'd meant it. But also feeling a bit guilty at the unspoken truth.

His stomach still tumbled in knots. He also wanted nothing more than to stay here. With Lune. He also wanted to escape this frightening unfamiliarity. Dive back into the old comfort of misery and grief.

He didn't want to talk about this anymore, so he searched for another avenue of conversation. He marveled at the light of the cloud-studded starscape coming through the large, round window. "The night sky," he whispered into the awkward silence. "Incredible."

"Surely you've seen stars before." Lune's tone was half amusement and half disbelief.

"Of course. But I was hoping to deter the direction of our chat."

Did Narsus imagine that quiet snort? Did Lune find him amusing? Narsus didn't know how that made him feel.

Obviously his ploy worked, for he heard Lune settle down into sleep.

Relieved at the growing silence, Narsus wondered if he'd been too callous and abrupt. Too honest. It was an awkward gap that left him alone with his thoughts.

Lune wasn't ready to drift off to sleep. He wondered if it was the serene and rhythmic rush of the waves outside that encouraged Narsus to express his feelings. He wasn't about to press, though.

He could sense Narsus was wide awake, watching the sky with him in quiet companionship. As the clouds grew thicker and the stars faded, the sky lit up with another round of rain and lightning. Just as he was about to drift off to sleep, Narsus's soft rustling alerted him. Narsus had turned over, facing the bundling board.

Lune half-opened his eyes to find Narsus watching him. Slowly, the phoenix reached out and placed an open palm against his side of the bundling board, gloved fingertips just cresting over the edge. After a moment, Lune turned to face him.

In the shadowed darkness, Narsus's green eyes glittered. Lune wasn't sure if it was from silent tears or not, and he wouldn't break the candid, reflective mood to ask. Narsus was showing himself willing to try, and Lune was glad. Because he wanted desperately to try, too. Careful not to touch the spread gloved fingers seen just above the wood, he placed his hand just adjacent to it, on his side.

"Lune?"

He was almost afraid to answer. Because this could be a dream. "Yes?"

"I'm—still unsure about all this. I've been mulling over the coincidences of the ways we've been brought together. Given I've said that, would you be receptive to me acknowledging our fated match? Of wanting to see if we can work with this Compass-partnership gifted to us? I'm—willing to try."

"And to see if there could be something in addition to that?" Lune had to moisten his lips and breathe against the pounding of his heart. The seconds were ticking by. Then a minute.

"I've come to our bed," Narsus said slowly. "You're kind, and so generous. More forgiving than anyone I've met. And, I am attracted to you."

Lune held his breath. This could work out after all. His dreams and desire for love, a family of his own, were within his grasp.

Fingers pressing harder into the bundling board, Lune replied, "I would welcome you, Narsus of the Verdigris. And I accept you as more than a Compass-mate—if that's something you'd like to explore."

Chapter 10

LUNE HAD FOUND IT difficult to sleep because of his excitement. So before dawn broke, he was up, sweeping the water out of the parlor, and wiping the furniture dry. Even the fourth jewel winking out could not tank his mood, but he made a mental note to consult Narsus about it when he awoke.

The joyful tune in Lune's heart had him humming, then singing a song he'd often hear in the village during festivals. It was a happy story about a boy making friends with coral fish. He always pretended the song was about him because it made him happy.

Cracking the eggs Narsus's friends had purchased from the neighbor down the road, Lune was getting into the tune with dancing. When he spun around and restarted the chorus, he nearly shrieked in surprise.

All three men—Narsus, Brightside, and Cinder were standing in the kitchen doorway. Staring at him. But only Brightside and Cinder's eyes were half-mast and glazed over. Pining admiration lingered there.

"So this is a siren's song?" Narsus asked, glancing from his entranced friends and back to him.

"Technically, no," Lune said sheepishly. "Calico's nudged me enough over the years, so I'm able to keep it in check. Mostly. But tones of it did slip in. It cements what I've been trying to tell you. That we're Compass-matched, because you seem immune."

"Imagine that," Narsus said, more to himself.

Lune smirked at the puzzled look on his Intended's face. More proof they were compatible. It was just taking Narsus a little more time to get used to the idea.

"Sooo...um." Narsus motioned at his friends. "Shouldn't you, uh. Undo your thing?"

Lune cursed at himself. "Right. Sorry." Filling a glass from the faucet, he approached the duo. Dipping his fingers in, he flicked the cold water into each man's face. He'd done this to Calico a few times over the years, so this remedy should work. "Wakey, wakey."

Brightside was the first to speak. His disapproval was cool and brisk. "You're a siren. We thought you were one of the more common of breed Mer-folk. Singing such a way wasn't very nice."

"I apologize. It comes too naturally." Lune held up the pan of scrambles in apologies. "Eggs?"

Cinder watched the exchange with curious energy, his eyes full of good-natured forgiveness. It helped dispel Brightside's brief show of displeasure.

"It wasn't done on purpose, I'm sure," Narsus defended. "I thought the singing very talented," he said to Brightside.

"Of course you would," the elf replied with neutral amusement.

"I agree." Cinder collected linen serviettes from the drawer. "He didn't do it on purpose. No harm was done. And we are uninvited guests in his home."

Brightside only scoffed with lukewarm upset and sat at the breakfast table. "May I have my eggs over well?"

"Of course you may," Lune replied brightly, turning back to the stovetop.

Cinder gathered plates and forks. "Scrambled is fine for me. Oh, and Nar prefers his dry. Very dry. Poor little dehydrated proteins."

The silence crackled so tensely, Lune turned to look. Narsus and Brightside stared at Cinder with wide, shocked expressions before looking at each other, then hiding said expressions.

"How do you know how I like my eggs?" Narsus demanded.

Cinder just shrugged and looked puzzled.

More silence.

Lune knew he had to break this weird tension. "Ah, if I may, may I see your compasses? Are there differences in designs?"

Only Cinder's compass made a brief appearance. It was around his neck. The phoenix lifted it into view as he salted his meal, but kept it close to his person. Lune didn't blame him. His own compass was a part of him. His very self. To be parted from it was soul-crushing. Just the thought of it made Lune check that it was still attached to his belt.

"They're all pretty much the same on the outside." Cinder tucked it back behind his shirt for safekeeping. "With the pattern on the shell case matching your birthmark. It's what's inside that counts. Inside, within the cogs and magic, is the essence of your Intended."

Narsus seemed to be very interested in his buttered toast and wouldn't look up. Brightside glanced at Narsus before toying with his linen serviette. "I lost mine when I was a child," the elf announced. "Our ship went down during a storm, within view of Temple Prime, thank the gods, so no one perished. I've hired divers over the centuries, but I fear it is gone for good."

"That's terrible!" Lune cried, his hand absently gripping his compass and worrying at it. "I'm so sorry."

Subdued, Brightside nodded cordially and nibbled at dry toast. Lune felt terrible for bringing up such painful memories. Suddenly aware of what he'd been doing, he yanked his hand off his compass. Clutching it like that in front of Brightside was unkind and rude.

"I'm...sorry," Lune repeated, softer now. "But wouldn't the magic preserve the compass?" he pressed. "You shouldn't lose hope. It could still be out there. Somewhere."

"Yes, the compass is intact," Brightside clarified. "The magic keeps it that way—usually. I meant I'll never see it again."

Lune detected the grief beneath the cool and collected elf-facade. Maybe because Lune knew how much his own compass meant to him. "Once Sachin gets back, I can take the Jade Raptor out and dive for it myself."

Narsus lifted his head, his fists tense on the table. "You have a boat? Named *Jade Raptor?*"

Cinder leaned over, giving Narsus an eyebrow wiggle. *"Jade Raptor.* Again, what more proof do you want?"

"*The* Jade Raptor," Lune corrected before turning to Brightside. "I can stay down indefinitely, so it's no problem to search."

Brightside lifted a hand, signaling Lune to contain his enthusiasm. "I apologize. It's lost forever. It happened over three centuries ago. Perhaps washed further out or found by treasure hunters."

"Oh." Lune deflated.

"I have learned to live with it," Brightside said.

Narsus slammed down his fork. It clattered loudly against his plate. "If you'll excuse me." He pushed back his chair and left the table.

"What?" Lune asked, confused. What had he done wrong? They'd been so agreeable yesterday and last night. Maybe he'd been too pushy with Brightside, and it upset Narsus.

Brightside too, put his fork down, but it was done with grace and care. "I've noticed you looking at him since we arrived. Searching for it. He doesn't have it."

"W-what happened to it?"

"He is the one who should relay that tale." Brightside and Cinder pardoned themselves from the table, collecting the abandoned meals as they went. Leaving Lune to stare at the last bits of breakfast on his plate.

·♥·♥·♥·♥·♥·

Narsus fell onto the sand, gripping it as it squeezed through his fists. His heart was squeezing, too. He was far enough away from the beach house where he felt safe enough to let his feelings flood. He knew now he'd made the biggest mistake of his life. Terror and loss raced through him at the realization.

Why? Why had he been so rash?

Lune was giving him chance after chance. Allowed him, and his friends to stay. Given him a place to sleep. Let him into his heart. Trusted him as an Intended should. And Narsus repaid that kindness by throwing away their mate-bond where he may never find it.

He had to try and find it before it was too late. And if it was too late, and the final jewel blinked out, would there be any way to fix it? Compass study classes said no, which spurred him on faster. Tearing off his clothes, he heard the frantic shouts behind him. It was Lune.

Unable to face his Intended, Narsus shifted into his phoenix form while running further up the beach. Determined to keep his poisoned body away from the fated mate he was willing to love.

"Wait!" Lune called. "Narsus, please! Where are you going?"

He didn't wait. He flapped his short, wide wings and took flight. He had to find it. He didn't want to make Lune cry. He didn't want to end up defeated and without hope like Brightside. He wanted to experience the love and life he'd been denying himself. With Lune. Before it was too late.

·♥·♥·♥·♥·♥·

Three more days had passed since Narsus had left the beach house without an explanation. In those three days, three more jewels had winked out.

That made seven in total that no longer shined. Lune clutched at his compass. He was doing his best not to panic, because doing so would only make it worse.

Rising concern had him showing the compass to Brightside and Cinder. Both men went pale and stricken. They turned away without a word.

Desperate, Lune grabbed at Brightside's sleeve. "Please. I'll beg if I have to. What does this mean? It's bad, isn't it. If it's so bad, why don't I sense it? Why doesn't the magic guide me like it did when it pointed me to the temple? Why are they blinking out every day? He's been looking for his compass, hasn't he? It's lost, like yours is."

Brightside cupped his cheek to calm him, then placed a hand to his shoulder. "Yes. He's trying to find it."

The confirmation didn't settle Lune any. "Why didn't he tell me? Or let me help? Doesn't he trust me? I thought we were coming to an understanding."

Brightside's grip tightened a little. "Lune, please calm down."

"I'll brew hot tea," Cinder piped up, worry flashing in those orange eyes. "I brought along the special kind. It'll help calm you." He darted into the kitchen.

"Thank you, but I don't want tea." Lune extracted himself from the elf. "Or to be calm. Now's not the time to be calm. I'm going back to the beach to wait for Narsus."

Storming out the door, Lune raced back to where he'd last seen his Intended. And stared at the scattered layer of rumpled clothing. Narsus's fears circled around Lune's resolve. Maybe he wasn't immune to the poison after all. But his fury was stronger than both their doubts combined. Because Narsus was immune to his siren's song. That alone gave Lune the courage to place even greater faith on the Compass-magic that bound them.

He gathered the clothes strewn around on the beach and folded them with care. He left them on a nearby rock in plain sight, so Narsus would find them with ease.

Within minutes of handling the garments, his hands tingled. Red and itchy spots appeared. His hands went numb. Lune groaned and refrained from scratching and screaming. Against his better judgment, he fell to his knees and thrust his hands into the layers of cool, gritty sand. It only made the itching flare up into fire. The sand began to puddle into glass shards.

Lune gasped, leaping to his feet as the infancy of green flames flickered here and there. The friction of the sand combined with the oils from Narsus's clothing had been the perfect combination. He felt the heat rising. *He was on fire!*

Wheezing and holding back screams, Lune's first thought was of his compass. He fumbled for it, holding it tightly with both hands. Clinging to it. Believing in it.

The flames seemed to abate, but the pain was still too intense. He needed Narsus, but self-preservation and instinct won out.

The water. His element would fix this. He'd hoped.

Lune raced into the surf, batting at the fire. The green flames thrived under the water, and the intense pain was rising. Panicking, hyperventilating, and thrashing, Lune wasn't aware of anything. Just the acute pains flashing through his entire body.

· ♥ · ♥ · ♥ · ♥ · ♥ ·

When Lune woke up, he was lying on the beach with the surf ebbing and flowing up to his gills. He gagged, pulling the hair away from the neck-flaps, and twisted the sopping wet strands into a loose pony-tail. He pinched his nose shut and blew sand from the gills to avoid further choking.

From the sun's position, he hadn't been unconscious for very long. He quickly checked his compass for confirmation. Yes. It was still just the seven days.

Lune pulled himself up and took stock of his hands. His skin was unblemished. With scales slowly fading back into the preferred husk of his human form. With an anxiety-filled look over his shoulder, he staggered to his feet. His legs felt like overcooked noodles, forcing him into a lurching, side-to-side gait until he regained his equilibrium.

He stopped to catch his breath, hands braced against both knees. His blouse and vest were slightly charred, and he had no trousers. Lune looked down at his legs. They were a pale, kind of glittery gray-purple-ly-mauve and blue. With scales. His elongated feet were quickly shrinking, turning back into toes instead of sturdy fins.

He'd...shifted into his siren form. And he'd been walking on two tails. Two legs. Two tails.

Lune felt his mouth split into a stupid, ear-to-ear smile. He'd shifted! Old expectations immediately crumbled. Maybe he had been missing out, having tails. He wanted to try shifting again.

Lune settled down on the warm, dry sand to steady himself while he concentrated. Biting his lip, he took a deep breath and held it precariously in his lungs. He thought about his legs reverting back into tails. Pictured it. Felt a warm heat building in his limbs.

His entire body violently twitched and bowed. A sharp pain rocketed through him. The sensation mirrored the agony of smashing his elbow against the table. Only it was everything going limp, numb, and tingly.

Following that, his gills burned, and he gasped for breath he couldn't catch. All the while momentarily losing his vision. Seconds turned into minutes. Minutes into more minutes before his body stopped torturing him, leaving him in a heaving, clammy sweat.

By Nolth, that was unpleasant.

Maybe it'd been too soon. Maybe shifting had a cool down period. He didn't know because he never bothered or cared to learn. But now he wanted to.

Examining his hands and legs again, he mulled over the experience of being in his natural state. Wondering if Narsus's flame had triggered his transformation, as some sort of defense or self-preservation. Wondering if the shock of this first shift had caused him to pass out from the stress, or if it was the panic of being on fire. Or maybe both.

But there was no evidence now of being burned. Or poisoned—ah, other than his missing trousers and torched blouse and belt. It was possible sirens had some measure of regenerative power. He wouldn't be surprised. Many other races had some ability to heal themselves or others. It wasn't anything that special. Calico's Breese phoenix forge had various levels of the healing gift.

Lune ran fingertips over the faint scars from the shark attack in his youth. What Calico hadn't been able to fix after that terror, Great Grandpa Acanthus had healed. Great grandpa had actually saved his arm. Lune let out a low noise and shook off the flashback. His excited mind had traveled too far back. Time to reverse and rethink.

Narsus's poison-fire. Then the sudden and unexpected appearance of his siren heritage. Scales that negated any burns. And toxicity. This just *had* to be even more evidence towards the truth of their Compass-paring. Lune shivered and giggled with anxious hope. They could do this. They could. None of this had been a dream.

Now, if only his fated mate would come home. So they could test this discovery. Together.

But first, trousers.

Chapter 11

NARSUS FLEW, CIRCLING THE cliffs below Temple Prime. Cliffs he felt great shame in revisiting. All he'd found were torn fishing nets and broken bottles.

It had been three long days since he'd made his mad dash from the kitchen. Terrified, he scrambled to remember the days, praying he was correct at seven. Technically, they were at the halfway point in the countdown. Or just past it, depending upon how precisely the magic itself worked.

He again scanned the craggy rocks and the breakers crashing against them. Marine life bobbed in the waves. The sun reflected off the whitecaps, drawing his attention to every glimmer he couldn't ignore, despite the fact his compass was too heavy to float.

Swimming in his Verdigris body was impossible. He would drown, and he didn't want to test just how undead he truly was. So he shifted back into his human body just before he hit the water. The turbulent chaos below the cliffs were a shock to Narsus's system, but he pressed on with his search.

No compass. No luck.

He'd resurfaced for air multiple times, only to plunge back into the depths. Using his phoenix flames to light up the sandy bottom. Through kelp fields and near tepid lava flows. Each mile he traveled yielded only more despair. Until he was too exhausted to make another dive. He didn't want to get too worn out that he wouldn't be able to pull himself out of the water.

Transforming back into his phoenix form, he gave a great heave of his wings, and flew back to his cliff-perch to dry off. Narsus didn't know why he thought he'd find it on the first, second, or even tenth attempt. It was likely he'd never see it again. Just like Brightside would never see his compass again.

Who had he been fooling? Thinking that he'd find it because he'd only chucked it a handful of days ago. It was time to confess. To ask Lune for the help he'd offered Brightside.

Maybe together, they could examine the bond he'd foolishly tried to escape.

Narsus prayed his Intended mate would forgive him if it was never found.

He braced himself against the harsh shoves of the coastal winds, huddling into the craggy rocks. *Oh gods. Oh, gods, what had he done?* He'd sabotaged himself. Destroyed hope by his own hand.

No. No, he had to have faith. There was still time. Lune's compass still had gemstones lit.

Brightside's words echoed in memory: *Fight, live!*

Narsus shook himself, striving to dispel sorrowful convictions that weighed him down like bricks. Waiting for the winds to dry his feathers to make flying easier.

He had always felt being Compass-born a burden. Now, he was experiencing separation anxiety at its loss. Not just with his compass, but with Lune himself. Even if their interactions were still forming.

The compass was their lifeline to each other. Like they'd already known each other for years. Perhaps they had. After all, Lune had poured his heart out to his compass for years. And in some way, Narsus had silently, reluctantly reciprocated.

With the failed hunt behind him, he knew he had to go home. To Lune. He'd been gone too long, and they had a lot to talk about. It was past time to offer his full trust. That was, if Lune still wanted it.

·♥·♥·♥·♥·♥·

Narsus found his clothes with the help of the glaring moonlight. The black garments were a beacon against the lighter-colored landscape. He had suspicions of who had folded them with care. But his churning gut was afraid to examine the hows of the deed in detail. And in what condition he would find that someone he was beginning to care about.

A couple hundred yards down the beach, he saw Lune was curled up and nearly in the surf. Staring up at the stars. The heat of the day had slightly abated. His siren had rolled down his sleeves and buttoned up that blue vest against the evening's ocean breeze.

Startled, Lune sat up at his approach, brushing off the wet sand and straightening his shirt and vest. They stared at each other in tense silence. Narsus knew they were both struggling through the hurt and awkwardness. Both afraid to make the first move in trying to salvage something that was barely even started.

Lune's eyes shimmered with upset. His, too, were glassy as he had to blot them with his scarf. Gentle, caring Lune, with the dusting of freckles across that bold, appealing nose. A land-stranded siren who'd given his all to this match. It was time Narsus stepped up to do the same, despite the grave fact they would never be able to touch.

Moving a little closer, Narsus stopped an arm-length away, holding the scarf over his nose and mouth lest he exhale unpleasant fumes. "If I worried you, I am so, so sorry."

His breath did hitch, and he fumbled to add another layer of linen protection over his face. "If I hurt you, I wish there was a way to take it back. Oh gods, I wish I could take it back. My behavior has been callous and cruel."

Lune opened his mouth to answer, but Narsus's sight blurred. "Please, let me finish. I can only pray you'll understand. And forgive me." He deliberately went to his knees. "I'll beg if necessary. Lune. I have to be honest. I—I threw the compass off a cliff before meeting you. I've been away. Trying to find it. I—I haven't been able to find it."

Lune's shoulders were set back and his full lips were flattened into a straight line. "I suspected something like that. Brightside wouldn't say exactly how it got lost. I've been thinking about it since you left. Why do such a thing?"

Narsus swayed slightly as he struggled to voice the truth. "I was afraid. Terrified. Certain that we wouldn't have a chance together, so it wasn't even worth the pain to try."

"Because you're a Verdigris."

Dejected, Narsus plopped down into the sand. The surf yanked at the edges of his cloak, sending it back, and forth.

"I'm going to hug you," Lune announced.

Surely, Narsus heard wrong. "W-what?"

"It's something you need right now, and I hope it'll be mutual. Will it, Narsus?"

Lune wanted to touch him? And prolong it? Even though he continued to disappoint this cheery, forgiving siren? This was his test. To himself, and to Lune. Narsus knew he had to forgive himself. To finally trust in their Compass-match. But could he? Really?

Narsus's heart swelled with agonizing grief. He couldn't breathe. Why was fear always hanging over him? Why couldn't he shake it? The words slipped out of his mouth. "No. Touching you. It's too dangerous."

Lune seemed to have courage enough for both of them. For his Intended rose to the challenge. "I handled your clothing when you flapped into your phoenix form."

Narsus startled himself with an anxious half-laugh. It alleviated some of the stress. "Flapped into my phoenix form?"

"Say that three times fast." Lune grinned, holding up his hand, palm up. "I forgive you, Narsus. We can work through this. There's still time. And even when the time does run out, we'll figure it out."

Narsus felt lightheaded that he even considered allowing a hug. He felt cowardly. Brave. Reckless. Stupid. Harmful. As if a part of him was hanging on by his fingernails, hoping. Even though he knew it could never be. "Don't you dare move. Not a muscle."

"I promise, Nar."

Nar. An endearment picked up from Brightside and Cinder. Still, he found he liked it coming from Lune. Narsus crept a little closer until he could smell the brine, the coolness of the ocean radiating from Lune's skin. Narsus pulled the cowl up over his head. Adjusted the fabric guarding his face. He bent his taller form down and tenderly allowed his shielded cheek to rest against Lune's chest.

"I'll—I'll only be a moment," Narsus promised.

"No hurry."

"No, I dare not linger." Narsus squeezed his eyes shut and did his best to hold back tears. This. This was friendship and trust of the highest honor. And he was grateful.

"Linger all you want, sweet Narsus."

And he did.

The eager press of another warm body. The quiet weight. The muted intimacy of it was addictive, and all so strange. Yet felt so right. It was only seconds later a terrible ache sprang inside Narsus's jaw. His chin trembled. A sharp sting of relief and grief traveled up his neck, and chased the emotional ache.

He was actually touching another living being.

Someone who cared about him. Someone he was experiencing great affection for. No. Not merely a someone. Lune. His fated mate. Lune, who forgave him, who was willing to fight to be with him. To love him.

The tears Narsus shed soaked into his scarf. A damp path trailed beneath the fabric of his throat. Blotting them back into the linen only made them pool further into the fibers. He was shaking at the stress, the overstimulation of it all. Narsus told himself to let go. To retreat, but he found himself hugging tighter. Not wanting this contact, this new connection, this comfort, to end. He didn't know a hug could ever feel this warm and tender. This safe.

The bawling and sobs assaulting his ears were coming out of his own mouth. He couldn't stop it. With each hitch of his breath, his body rocked in response. Before leaning into the strength of his Compass-mate's stance. Lune was braced like one of the mighty deity statues that surrounded the grounds of Temple Prime, despite Narsus being so much taller.

Narsus didn't know when, but soon found that he was no longer shaking. Lune's heartbeat was a slow, calming thump against his ear. Narsus listened to it, allowing himself to feel the love and companionship that was willingly offered.

"Th-thank you. For holding me," Narsus whispered before pulling far away, and immediately feeling the suck of loneliness once again. "For k-keeping your promise to not move." The grief of this simple separation didn't emotionally hurt as much as he thought it would. Because he knew Lune wasn't going to go away.

Narsus wiped his eyes again, this time with the excess material of his cowl. Lune sat down, pretending not to notice by drawing whimsical lines in the sand. Lines that curved into hearts. This tender act of kindness made Narsus realize how much more painful it was to exist without love. But no matter how much he and Lune cared for each other, Narsus still feared skin-to-skin contact would be out of the question.

"I-I'm sorry for carrying on like a child."

"I'm not," Lune said. "You've honored me with such deep and intimate trust. As fitting between Intendeds."

The reply should have embarrassed him further. But right now, all Narsus wanted to do was surrender, and *feel*.

"Lune?" His voice was ragged, gritty. Desperate. "May I have another hug?"

Lune reclined in the dry sand, away from the surf, and outstretched his arms in welcome.

Chapter 12

THE SEAGULLS WERE SQUAWKING. Waves were crashing, and the sun was shining. Lune awoke to find his face nested into his pillow, and he had no recollection of how he got here. Was it possible Narsus had carried him to bed? The thought of Narsus's large hands on him made his cheeks go rosy, and he shook off the delicious, giddy shiver. There was a brief disappointment that he was still fully dressed. But baby steps.

Tucking hair behind his ears, a gleam of metal caught his eye. His joy instantly fizzled. His compass was on the nightstand.

Lune didn't need to look to know an eighth jewel had gone dark. He could sense the hollow emptiness of it now.

The closer he got to Narsus emotionally, the compass's warning would only wrap around his heart with more urgency. But he worried bringing it up would crush the courage Narsus was just starting to find.

Lune also worried about dumping too many expectations on his Intended at one time. Narsus was just starting to accept their Compass-pairing, and learning to be kind—especially to himself. Lune so desperately wanted Narsus to be kind to himself. To forgive himself.

He also wanted to tell Narsus that there was a chance his siren form made him immune to that magnificent verdant flame. And that he was having a bit of a learning curve summoning up his tails again.

He'd have to play these issues by ear.

More importantly, they had to discuss exactly when and where Narsus had discarded the compass. There were so many possibilities of its location. It could be wedged between the rocks. Or be in pieces. It could be buried in the sediment by the force of the current, or entangled in a bed of seaweed. Where ever it was, together they'd find it.

Lune turned, ready to knock politely upon the bundling board. It was imperative they start the day renewing their budding relationship.

But Narsus's side of the bed was empty.

There was a note on the pillow. Lune grabbed it.

Dear Lune,

Ah gods, last night, you gave me a heart and soul I will greedily guard forever. Your tenderness and devotion isn't something I deserve, but I will work hard to earn your forgiveness. I know I'll be forever groveling for my massive mistake. I've stained not just myself, but us.

The fault is mine that I might have permanently destroyed what has brought us together. All because of my previously identified self-worth. The guilt is something I will live with to the end of my days.

The only thing I want more than waking up beside you every day, is to find my compass. I dream of being able to touch you without barriers. To feel the coolness of your skin, even though we both know it cannot be.

You know where I've gone. I will return just after nightfall.

Yours, Narsus

Lune bowed his head and pressed the letter against his temple. Not knowing if he should be flattered at the sweetly awkward attempt at romance. Or be angry. Narsus had gone off without him, again, frantically searching for what he'd foolishly thrown away. Determined to fix the tragic mistake he'd made, without help from anyone.

If Lune had known where Narsus had lost it, he would've just set out to join him. When would his dear, adorable little bird-brain phoenix-mate understand it no longer had to be that way? What Narsus said about touch was disconcerting. But Lune put that dilemma aside for another time.

When Narsus returned, they would have words. Because the letter hinted at that dark something sprouting from those Compass-jewels. In the meantime, he'd have to keep busy instead of sitting here worrying and stewing. Carefully folding the note, Lune slipped it into a drawer atop the ones Calico had written him.

Throwing on some fresh clothes, he found he had the house to himself. A note on the kitchen table told that Brightside and Cinder had taken the farmer's recommendation to visit the next town over. Probably for that fancy bookstore. So he knew they'd probably left by sun up.

That left him free for the rest of the day.

Which brought his thoughts back to Narsus. He should do something to cushion the harsh words he had for his fated mate, but what?

A present. A seashell. A green turbo shell he'd take to the jeweler to polish. He'd have to pay extra for the rush work, of course. He'd have to hurry himself, if he was going to get back before Narsus.

He sprinted out of the beach house and into the water. The bubbles of his dive rose, bouncing and popping. The muted hums of the ocean itself alive within him, churning, vibrating. Above, the muffled realm of the dry world grew dimmer. When he reached the bottom, the vibrations of the depths sharpened as he adjusted to his natural element. The sensations tickled his skin, further awakening his aquatic senses.

Lune froze. A flashback of the shark attack in his youth throttled his progress. A tinge of fear spread through him. Quickly, he plucked a tie from his pocket to anchor the hair away from his face and gills. Then looked out into the surrounding waters. Still nothing. His shoulders relaxed. Just traces of past trauma messing with his head.

Lune pulled himself along the sandy floor and found a sharp rock, just in case. It was better than nothing, and he couldn't allow his fears to stop him. Because Narsus needed him. His Intended was trying so hard. Lune wondered what more he could do to reassure his mate.

Gifting the shell as a wedding present came to mind. Lune's eagerness and excitement made him quiver. It would need to be of a good size and color. One with at least three whorls, or sections, to represent the stages of their struggles—Narsus's struggles.

Searching among the corals and crevices brought him many specimens, but they weren't quite right. Either too small, or after a thorough examination, wouldn't be green after a polish. As he went along, he sustained himself by cracking oysters and choking down the gross, slimy meat. He hated eating it, but his body was made for it, and there was no way he'd waste time by breaching the surface to get a more palatable meal.

Time passed quickly, and the hour was getting late. If he couldn't find Narsus's gift today—*there!* At the entrance of a crevice. It was a rough and gritty shell about the size of his palm. Covered in algae, so it would need extra attention. He picked it up, judging the color. Then examining the aperture for the snail. Empty. Possibly eaten by an eel or crab.

As if it had given up its life to belong to Narsus.

It seemed fitting for the son of the undead phoenix god. A destined tribute.

It was perfect.

Lune hurried back to the surface, racing into town in sopping wet clothes.

With assistance from magic, the crafter worked his skills about the shell. Lune watched each step, in essence, putting a little of himself into the process. From the first initial scrubbing. To the dousing with a cleansing acid. Washing and drying. Filing, grinding, sanding. Buffing and polishing it with mineral oils.

Lune's excitement bubbled as the textures and patterns emerged. A mid-tone green color was prominent. Thin lines of a rust-red brown accented the shell. As if to declare that Narsus's undead heritage had merged into his Verdigris one.

For a final touch, Lune requested a pearly band carved into the shell's pattern. With a final polish, it was ready. Complementary wrapping was accepted. With the sun already dipped into the ocean and dusk falling, Lune rushed home.

Chapter 13

Lune found Narsus in the kitchen fixing a sandwich.

Brightside and Cinder were nowhere in sight, but Lune noticed the lights blazing from his childhood room. This privacy was perfect timing.

Sliding into one of the tall chairs, Lune leaned over the island counter. "Hi."

Narsus looked up from his task. "Hi."

The slow, despondent movements of the sandwich creation, and the expression on his mate's face said it all. Lune fought the urge to reach out and console.

"I didn't find it," Narsus confessed, his tone low.

The stern lecture Lune had planned poofed out of existence. Narsus didn't need to hear it. "There's plenty of days left, see?" Lune held out his compass to show off the five jewels that were still lit. "Tomorrow, we'll go together," he offered lightly, but hiding the leashed panic within. "We'll find it then. They're beacons to each other, aren't they? So it'll be okay."

Narsus's head shot up and his eyes went wide. "What did you say?"

Lune was just as startled. "W-what? You mean they aren't? But isn't that how we're supposed to find each other? I chased you all around Temple Prime during past festivals. For years. You used yours to avoid me—you can't convince me you didn't. So the magic's certainly more sophisticated than just luring us to a marriage ceremony."

Narsus just stared at him. And stared some more. Until, "N-no—you're correct. They are...beacons. ...To each other." Then his gaze slowly darted around as that information sunk in. Not looking anywhere in particular, but thoughts focused inward.

Elbows braced on the counter, Narsus covered his face with his hands. Relieved sobs and hitches cascaded. Lune didn't have to be an empath to sense the waves upon waves of grief and gloom washing away. Decades of it. Maybe centuries. He wanted so badly to wrap his arms around those heaving shoulders. But he dared not touch without permission.

When the sobbing began to taper off, Lune fetched a tea-towel and offered it. Narsus wiped his eyes before tucking the linen away in a pocket.

"Thank you. Five days left. But with your compass to track mine, it feels like all the time in the world has been given back to us."

Wanting so badly to wrap Narsus in a hug, Lune rested his palms on the table instead. Responding not by asking to touch, but comforting his Intended with his gaze alone. His mate had gone through enough emotional turmoil for the night.

"Did Brightside and Cinder eat yet?" Lune could tell Narsus was grateful for the new avenue of conversation.

"Uh...yeah." Narsus fiddled with the crumbs scattered around from slicing bread. "They're exhausted from all the sun, fresh air, and walking. They retired with the armloads of books they bought. We won't see them for a while. I just might have to do a kitchen-to-bedroom door delivery to see if they're still alive, later. Although I'm sure they spied on me sobbing like a baby just now."

Lune snacked on the bits of discarded tomato left on the cutting board. "I'm sure they did. They seem like good friends."

"They are."

"They'll be fine," Lune assured. "But I'm thankful they left us alone."

Narsus glanced at him again, endearingly shy and demure, but returned to constructing the abandoned sandwich. "I agree. I...think that was the bulk of their plan. To get us together. Do you want half?"

Narsus was already slicing the snack in two. Lune watched, concealing his sympathy that his Intended wore gloves just to throw together a simple meal.

"It would be nice to share." Out of sight, Lune fiddled with the shell, making sure the tissue paper was still neatly wrapped after removing it from his pocket. "Narsus? I have something for you. A present." Lune was both happy and saddened at the renewed surprise that flit across his mate's face.

Narsus nervously reached atop his head for the beaked mask that wasn't there. "What's the occasion? I-I haven't gotten you anything. I've been nothing but horrid and disrespectful to you."

"That wasn't intentional, Nar. You were only protecting yourself. You've realized how harmful that was. To yourself. Me. And everyone else. You've been genuinely remorseful. Trying very hard to achieve clarity and reflection."

Narsus stared at the sandwich. After a few seconds, he plated the two halves and slowly slid one across the counter. "Sharing a snack doesn't seem like an equal exchange."

Lune shrugged. "Healing takes time. Marriages aren't always equal. It's a partnership where you take care of each other. Sometimes that means a less than equal footing. But that's what we're here for. To lean on each other during times of stress, or just when you're trying to sort it all out."

"How did you get to be so knowledgeable about such things?"

Lune grinned. "Calico."

"Ah, yeah, that explains it. Grandfather was always the balancing force."

Lune place the gift on the table, watching Narsus's dark green eyes light up with eager wonder. Narsus timidly reached out, his fingers stroking the crinkly tissue. As if memorizing the moment, the gesture. Until he could wait no longer. The binding bow unraveled, and the paper rustled as it was pushed back.

Lune went nervous as Narsus just stared at it. He was unable to read his mate's expression. "I hope it's okay."

"It's...green." Narsus said, still staring, transfixed. "A sparkly, magical mix of several shades of green."

"I'll find you a different color, if you want." Lune was starting to feel that maybe this wasn't the best idea. He reached out to take it, but Narsus beat him to it, with a speed that was incredible.

"Don't you dare." Holding it protectively to his chest, Narsus rushed out, "It's beautiful. The pearly white band just makes the greens pop." He reverently traced the textures and lines. "As if showing me the path out of the darkness of what I am. I'm so touched at how much thought you put into this."

Lune was shocked when Narsus came around the counter and hugged him without hesitation. Lune was obedient, holding still as previously instructed, especially since Narsus's scarf wasn't concealing his nose and mouth.

The embrace was extremely short-lived, but Lune treasured it just the same. For it had been given willingly and without prompting.

"Green was always a burden in some way to me. My least favorite color, because of what I am—until now. Lune?" Narsus turned to him. "You've seen that I can shine. I want to shine. For you."

"We'll shine together, Nar," Lune whispered. "Together."

In silent agreement, they brought their sandwiches into their room. Lune felt a little anxious over the intimacy of it. Even though with the discovery of his siren-shifting and the mystery of the Compass-jewels looming on the horizon. They'd figure it out. Soon.

But not when Narsus was further opening up to him. One beautiful step at a time. The burdens that needed to be spoken could wait. Just a bit longer.

·❤·❤·❤·❤·❤·

They were sitting cross-legged on the bed, facing each other. With the bundling board securely between them. Narsus was having a difficult time accepting this happiness. He wanted to grasp it with both talons and hang on for dear life. And this sea shell was the heart of it, his point of entry.

He balanced his gift on one knee, with the sandwich plate on the other. Lazily alternating his attention between Lune and the shell. His fated mate had taken the time to give him a present. The joy of it did funny things to his gut.

When they were done eating, Narsus moved his shell to a place of honor on his nightstand. Close to the wall peg that displayed his beaked mask. The mask. The symbol of his safety. His ability to hide both himself and others from harm. It kept Lune from harm.

There was a gentle knock upon the bundling board. "Would you cuddle with me again?"

There must have been a look of terror on his face, for Lune tried to calm him. "You can stay cocooned in your fabric fortress if you'll be more comfortable."

"Maybe," Narsus rushed in a sharp, defensive tone. He quickly held up his hands. "Sorry. I'm...trying. It's still all so new and a bit overstimulating if I dwell on it too much. Even though I crave it."

"Shhh, I know. It's okay." Dusting the crumbs off his fingers, Lune put the plate on his bedside table. "May we remove the bundling board? We'll be more comfortable."

Narsus was already working at the latch. Then he removed himself from the bed. Lune took care of his end, and returned the offending barrier to the closet. Unsure of what Lune wanted him to do, Narsus waited as his Intended climbed in and spread himself out right in the middle.

Nervously, Narsus yanked the scarf up over his nose and mouth. "What were you thinking of doing?"

"Another cuddle workshop. Or groping if you want to get naughty—"

"Naughty?" Narsus snorted. The instant idea of tit-for-tat zipped through his brain. He tempered his vocal cords to mimic Calico's voice and inflections. Then answered with: "There shall be none of that. No talking like Calico, please. That's not something I need in my head when we're in our bed."

Lune just stared at him, shocked eyes figuratively as big as dinner plates. Then his mate busted out a raucous laugh. Lune even had to hold his belly he was shaking so hard. Narsus couldn't help the smile that stretched across his mouth. Seeing Lune laugh was... Narsus had to steady his ragged breathing.

Lune suddenly stopped laughing and blinked those expressive brown eyes. He pursed those full lips that slightly twitched that large, attractive nose. Narsus couldn't stop drinking in the sight. Then a worried expression flittered over Lune's face. Following that expression was a pillow whomping Narsus in the shoulder.

Snapping his mind away from carnal thoughts, Narsus demanded, "Why'd you hit me?" Although he already figured out *why* it happened.

"*That* was a fun surprise." Lune wiped away the jovial tears. "But you used contractions and weren't proper and stuffy enough. But yeah, yeah, I get it. I'll do my best to rein in any Cal-isms. Especially here."

Another swing of the pillow mussed up Narsus's hair this time. "And this one is for getting ahead of yourself," Lune continued. "Ogling me like some sort of dessert. I'm quite aware phoenix run passionately too hot."

Narsus followed when Lune jumped off the bed. They chased each other around, laughing, shouting. Crashing into the bookcase, causing it to thump and rattle against the wall. Several knickknacks rolled to the floor with yet another clatter, but did not break.

"Oops," Lune giggled, shoving the items closer to the wall with his foot. "You don't think we're attracting unwanted attention, do you?"

Narsus halted, listening, then shook his head. "Bree's a telepath, and an empath. They won't bother us."

Lune wrinkled his nose with a mischievous grin. Then stalked forward. "Good."

Narsus tensed at the bit of fluff held above Lune's head, and lunged to secure his own pillow. He lifted it and sent a swing back. And missed.

Hooting and laughing, Lune jumped back up on the bed. "It's about damn time you picked that up. I was starting to wonder. Let's get rid of some of that pent-up energy."

"So you're saying I'm slow?" Narsus asked, half-offended, but full surprise radiating from the question.

"With your aim, and your perchance at having fun."

That did it. "Perchance?" Narsus teased in reply. "That's such a Calico word. Did you even use that correctly in a sentence?"

Lune puckered his lips like a fish and shrugged with utter indifference.

Narsus aimed the next swing at Lune's knees. His mate shrieked at the swift, harmless contact, dropped to his butt, and rolled off the opposite side of the bed. Narsus crawled over the rumpled sheets in pursuit.

Their laughter rang throughout the suite as they took turns chasing each other back and forth across the mattress. Even under it in a hail of muffled giggles. They skipped around in circles about the washroom, leaping over the narrowest stretch of the sunken bath.

It was nearly a joint, mutual surrender inside the walk-in closet. Until a well-placed smack tore a seam of the soft cushion. Feathers and down arced out and floated in the air. More squeals, more warm hilarity orchestrated them back to the main room, where they collapsed upon the bed.

Both heaving from the exertion.

Narsus was dizzy and worn out with joy. He was barely able to spit a stray feather off the corner of his mouth because his body was so comfy and cushy in this big bed.

There was a dip, a flop, and the mattress bounced several times. Narsus barely opened an eye to spy Lune fussing, trying to get comfortable. Perhaps still wound up with excitement.

Knowing he was safely cocooned in his gloves and long sleeves, Narsus reached out to wrangle his still overly-animated mate. A mate who'd knocked the wind out of his sails, and left this silly undead poison phoenix in a pile of exhausted feathers.

It was a shock when Narsus realized he'd scooped Lune up into his arms. Plopping him against his chest to still the wiggling. Narsus was met with a low, wicked chuckle.

"I got you right where I want you," Lune announced.

Narsus rumbled with lazy mirth. "You had me here before."

"Ah, but you're more relaxed now, am I right?"

"You're so right," Narsus agreed, his voice going gritty and lethargic. Savoring the ragged, heaving, uneven flow of them catching their breath. Their hearts thumping in response to that fun, spontaneous romp. He was super relaxed, despite Lune snuggling up against him, pressing his nose into the heavy fabric of his woolen tunic.

"Mmmm. You smell of coals and fire," Lune mumbled against his chest. "I love it. It's natural. Fresh. Manly. Reminds me of campfires on the beach during group dates when I was a teen. Our family's scents are all so stuffy and cloying and fussy. As much as I love Cal, his chosen scents often gave me low grade headaches."

Narsus's eyes flashed wide, but he didn't move. Or let on that the comments had caught his interest. So Lune was aware of phoenix holding certain scents close to their hearts. Just how far did his mate's knowledge go? Had Calico shared their secrets with Lune? He'd wait for additional dropped details before inquiring over the matter further.

At this moment though, the warm weight of Lune's body snuggled up against him took precedence. It was all so new. Strange. Comforting. Frightening. It was a fear and sensation Narsus welcomed.

And at this present moment, Lune visibly inhaling, enjoying that smoky essence of his phoenix-self, carried Narsus to a place where grief didn't exist.

Chapter 14

"CINDER! LUNE!"

Narsus's screams had Lune scrambling to his knees from a dead sleep. He squinted at the bright light filling the room. Green flames engulfed the bed. The fire licked across the walls and ceiling.

And danced up his arms.

Screaming himself, Lune slapped at his body until he realized he wasn't being hurt. Just dripping sweat and excessively uncomfortable at being wrapped within this flickering element. Further jarred by Narsus's sobs, Lune realized a nightmare had summoned the flames.

He looked over, seeing Narsus still asleep, curled into a ball. Limbs pressed tight against his body and twitching without mercy. More cries, instantly growing into high-pitched, heaving wails.

Lune leaned over, trying to catch his breath from the shock and fright. He stopped cold at reaching out to touch. Narsus's beaked mask. Hanging on its peg above the nightstand. It glowed and pulsed, as if alive. Seemingly fed and awakened by the fire and reveling within it. Watching him. Judging him. This was the Grim's mask. A god's mask.

Lune shook off the hypnotic sight and seized his mate's shoulders.

"Narsus!"

Narsus's eyes flew open, and he quickly rolled to his feet. Away from the touch, and away from the bed. It took several more seconds for

Narsus to regain his bearings. Then, panicked, he immediately snuffed out every trace of the fire.

"Where?" Narsus demanded, rushing back to him. "Where are you burned?"

Lune hurried to find his voice. "I-I'm not." He held out his hands and arms for inspection, spying the trace of scales quickly fading away. Just like before. It was as he'd thought. His siren-self protected him. "Narsus, I'm immune to your flame."

"I...I could have killed you. Just like I killed—" Narsus's features crumbled and he turned away. "I'm sorry, I'm sorry."

The look of fear and shame that washed over his mate hurt Lune's heart. "Narsus, I'm all right."

His Intended pulled nervously at his green braid and glanced around the room. Lune had a feeling he was examining the magic spells painted into the suite. "No, it was Cal's magic that saved you. You're not immune."

Lune would argue about that much later. Right now, Narsus needed him. "Would you care to talk about your nightmare?"

"I...I told you. I hurt someone I cared about. They...died."

"Your first Compass-match?" Lune asked softly.

"H-how did you know?"

"I didn't. I figured that's the only person you'd even consider let getting close to you."

"It wasn't a match," Narsus said, sitting tensely on the edge of the mattress. "It was a magic hiccup that got someone killed."

Lune sat a few inches away from him. "It destroyed your ability to trust in the compass. And yourself."

Narsus covered his face. "We—we thought since we were both phoenix, my poison wouldn't be a problem."

Lune frowned. "He was a phoenix? Why would you think that?"

"Ah, gods, Lune," Narsus rushed. "I'm sorry. It's something I can't get into—"

A harried knock on the bedroom door had them both tense. It was Cinder who called out. "Narsus, Lune, I'm coming in!"

The door flew open. Orange flames lapped around Cinder's body, and his hair and eyes burned with his natural element. "We smelled smoke, and felt the heat," he said.

Narsus only grunted and turned away. Several hitches of grief escaped before he was able to control himself. Lune flinched at his mate's acute response.

"Narsus?" Cinder asked, and started further into the room.

Lune pushed off the bed, blocking the approach. Eager to take the attention off Narsus, and experiencing a little bit of possessive jealousy. Because he'd witnessed the same lovelorn looks on the faces of his old school chums in the past. And right now, both men seemed to be wearing it.

"We're okay, Cinder. Narsus put out the flames. I'm not hurt. Thank you, but we're fine now."

The other phoenix wasn't retreating. Only staring at Narsus with a weird expression straining his face. Jealousy within Lune started to build a bonfire of its own.

"Cinder, they're well," Brightside stepped into view, drugged with sleep and night robe askew. The elf suddenly straightened up taller and quickly tried to rub the sleep out of his eyes. "Cinder, recall your flame."

The orange phoenix did so, and that was when the elf took ahold of his arm. "Lune, I apologize," Brightside said. "My fault. I sent him in here in case he needed to put out a fire. I wouldn't have done it if it hadn't been an emergency. I should've realized Cal would have safeguards on his—your house."

"It's...fine," Lune said faintly. Narsus mentioned Brightside was an empath and a telepath. Was the elf reacting to the rising tension between the two phoenix? It only made what was playing out more suspicious.

"Goodnight, then," the elf said. Kindly but firmly, Brightside yanked a stunned Cinder out of the room and shut the door.

Only then did Narsus lift his head. He grabbed the beaked mask from its peg and put it on. "Lune? I—I need some air. Stroll the beach with me?"

"Of course." His heart quickened. Narsus wasn't pushing him away.

They'd walked in silence. Back and forth through the ebbing and flowing surf. Frantic, at first, sending up splashing waves with each footfall. Lune followed quietly behind, allowing Narsus his space. Then they lounged on the beach; Lune sitting close beside his mate in silent support, but not touching.

Narsus's breathing had returned to normal so that it no longer sounded as rough coming out of that beaked mask. His body had relaxed into the consistency of a wet noodle. The gentle rounds of controlled inhales and exhales had done its job. As did the serene roll of the surf.

Narsus's muffled voice gently pierced the night. "I'd thought I'd burned you alive. In my nightmare, I mean."

"A nightmare means you're still trying to work through this. Still trying to trust yourself, and the compass."

"Yeah," Narsus said after a minute. "I'm not sure I'm doing very well."

"You *are* doing very well," Lune corrected. "You've faced and conquered each step we've taken together."

"No, not all of them."

Lune pursed his lips. "You didn't just call out to me in your nightmare."

Narsus's heavy sigh signaled he knew. "And you've put two and two together."

"Yeah. Narsus? You said you'd killed him."

"I did. He was reborn. A common enough occurrence with my kind. But Lune, please. I can't...talk about it. I won't. I'm sorry."

Lune reached out across the sand, his hand stopping inches from Narsus's. "I *do* understand. And respect it."

Narsus turned to face him, watching him. Lune braved the piercing stare of those darkened lenses. Until Narsus said, "You *do*, don't you?"

"I was raised by a phoenix, remember?"

A few seconds passed between them. Then, Narsus's hand inched across the sand to meet his. Slowly, their fingers entwined, and Narsus's beaked mask turned back toward the stars shining above.

Chapter 15

"I CAN SHARE WHAT I know about phoenix," Lune announced into the peaceful, warm night. "If it'll help you open up to me."

Narsus's beaked mask turned to him again, but only briefly, before he looked back up into the sky.

Lune wondered what was racing through his Intended's mind right now, but he could guess. Because he was starting to feel the perspiration seep through Narsus's thick gloves. Lune was happy that Narsus seemed reluctant to let go of his hand. But he knew the nerves must be pretty bad on Narsus's end. Especially when the gloves were yanked off and absently flapped dry.

Narsus tucked his bare hands into the safety of his armpits. "I'm seriously interested to hear your stories."

Lune tried to contain himself, because that had been a shaky, but very eager response. "Even though Cal tried to get me to accept my watery heritage, I was raised phoenix."

There was a muffled snort inside the mask. "And exactly *why* would he do that?"

Lune shrugged. "He never really said. But I wonder about that, now that you're in my life. Most nights, Cal would transform into his flame-self. He'd tell me phoenix stories through his telepathy. Always cautioning that these stories were for me only."

"Why?"

The question was urgent. The tone was nearly rasping. Lune rested his chin on his knees. "Because he was putting the trust—and life of an entire people in me. Because he believed in me that much. Right now, I'm thinking he believed in us, that much. To help you believe in me. Those personal scents. They're your lifelines. Your ability to remember who you are from life to life. It anchors you. Your sanity. Without them, you're vulnerable to harm from others."

"Yesss." The response Lune got was strangled. A hiss of grief. Maybe relief.

"Do you have a lifeline?" Lune asked quietly.

"No. I'm undead."

Lune didn't want to push in that direction. For the breathing grew distressed, ragged. "Do you have a true flame form?"

"All phoenix have a true elemental form. It takes experience and practice."

"May I see it?"

Another lengthy pause and silence had Lune worrying. Narsus shifted around in the sand, seemingly uncomfortable, then asked, "My elemental form?"

"Yes. Or is it another secret?"

"Not technically a secret, no."

"Then is it something personal and intimate? Only for the eyes of family?"

"No, not technically," Narsus repeated. "It's just that I'm a poison phoenix..." His voice trailed off.

"And you're afraid the poisons would be at their strongest through the fumes?"

"Maybe...I...don't know. It's been decades since I achieved that particular form. It's been unnecessary."

"How could you being you be unnecessary?" Lune turned to him. "Nar? Don't you want to stretch your wings and soak up that freedom?"

Narsus's posture went rigid. "Are you being sincere, or are you just wanting to see me naked again in my human form?"

Lune stretched his grin as far as it would go. "Both."

There was a brief silence before Narsus replied. "I can assure you the process is near instantaneous for the experienced."

"And you're experienced?"

"You won't catch sight of any exposed flesh, if that's what you were hoping."

"Still waiting," Lune singsonged.

With a chuckle, Narsus stood up, brushing the sand off his trousers. Stepping back several paces, and highlighted only by the moonlight, he dropped his cloak.

"Slower," Lune teased.

Narsus reached up for his mask. The hard leather casing hit the sand with a small thud. That's when Narsus froze. Staring at it, watching the shadows of his flame caressing the pristine leather.

"Nar?" Lune asked. "You don't have to do this if you don't want to."

Narsus met his gaze, and Lune witnessed the cascade of mixed emotions that lived there. "I'm surprised at how easy that was. Discarding it in your presence." He gestured to the mask.

Lune held his breath and said nothing. Not wanting to fracture the flow of his Intended's emotions and actions. There was a lot of thought rushing through those green eyes in these quick seconds. With the next blink, Lune knew decisions had been made.

Narsus's boots hit the sand. Maybe Lune should have said something. Because now Narsus was making a torturous game of it. With each button undone on those trousers, Lune was entranced, enjoying the private show.

The transformation was swift, swirling first into a cloud of dark smoke, then flashing into existence with a pop of writhing flames. Shimmering. Undulating. Glowing in several shades of green from lights to darks. Narsus looked similar to his corporeal phoenix form, only this one was brilliant, transparent. Airier, and his shape was streamlined, elongated.

Lune gasped at the grandeur, then erupted into defeated, amused chuckles. "You tease. I know you said it'd be a fast shift, but I wasn't expecting *that* fast."

Being able to see right through Narsus in this form should be unnerving. But it wasn't. The phoenix crest atop Narsus's head stretched back at least twice as long as the one on his physical phoenix body.

"Narsus." Lune's voice was a thready, breathy whisper. "Such raw beauty. You've displayed an even greater amount of trust in me. In us. *Thank you.*"

A gentle ripple cascaded through Narsus's fiery body. The glow of his green-white eyes softened. It encouraged Lune to make another request.

"Since we've gone this far," Lune said in a soft, neutral tone. "Become this vulnerable with me, I want to ask for yet another level of trust."

Lune crossed his legs and continued to sit in the sand. He was unsure if they could clearly communicate while Narsus was in this form, so Lune outstretched his hand, with the compass in it. "May I touch you?"

Narsus reared back, rising a few feet further into the air. His fear and surprise manifesting in the sudden, silent sparks of his fiery being. His wings shook, as if to emphasize the danger.

Lune strove for patience and love. "Yes, I know you're fire. I want to prove to you we're compatible. Trust in the compass's magic. You must know I'm the one who handled your garments on the beach that day."

Clouds of dark smoke puffed out of that transparent, fiery beak, followed by a low hiss and pop. It was Firespeak. It sounded the same as, yet so different from, the snaps and crackles emitting from Narsus's fire form.

Calico and other relatives spoke the elemental language from time to time. But if you weren't created of a flame's essence, you'd never be able to converse in it. Or understand.

And right now, Firespeak was the only way Narsus would be able to communicate. Unless...

"You wouldn't happen to be telepathic like Cal, would you?"

There was a toss of that fiery head, and then what looked like an exasperated stare.

So much for that idea. Lune would just have to guess his Intended's purpose. "Narsus...honestly, your poisons did blister my skin. But I shifted. Without realizing it. I got scales, and two really fun tails. My original siren-self negated any harm. And healed me."

Narsus's fire feathers fluffed out and burned brighter.

"Please," Lune begged. "I've been trying to get you to believe me."

The wispy, crackling element that was Narsus descended to the beach. The granular particles beneath his mate's clawed feet melted the sand into a smooth, flat puddle of molten glass.

Narsus huffed out caution with another dark ring of smoke. Still in his fiery bird form, he walked out of that puddle and onto the sand. It took several steps until the sand did not scorch and melt. Narsus then signaled permission by lowering his head.

Lune followed, minding where he placed his bare feet until he reached a safe zone. Even in his phoenix fire-form, Narsus was tall and intimidating—sexily so. The flames jumped toward Lune, licking along his fingers. He kept the compass between them. The heat was no hotter than a warm bath. His skin did not blister or catch.

After a few seconds, Narsus calmed even more. The phoenix crest turned from chaotic, jagged edges to smooth, round contours. The flames now mimicking the calm, rolling waves caressing the beach.

"I'm going to drop the compass a notch, keeping ahold of the chain," Lune said. "Are you willing?"

Narsus didn't move or protest.

Lune let the compass dangle upon its chain. There was no change in the level of heat. "I want to drop it. Not have it as a barrier. Are you still willing?"

Narsus didn't withdraw.

Filled with hope, Lune said, "Okay, dropping it now."

The compass hit the cool, grainy earth with a soft thud.

Nothing changed. Lune was still caressing the flames that were Narsus's wings. There was no pain, no burns or scarring. He held out his hands to show his Intended.

Narsus's flame fluffed up some more, and there was another crackle of Firespeak. Lune knew this time it was in joy and surprise. So Lune settled down across the sand. "Be with me. *Feel* with me."

The slow, calm undulations of his Intended's flame gave Lune his answer. At each flicker, the transparency faded into the opaque textures and patterns of real quills and feathers. From there, Narsus's human-self re-formed. Fully clothed.

Chapter 16

PULLING HIS SCARF OVER his nose and mouth, Narsus balanced onto his knees and toes. Hovering over Lune's prone form. Being this close to someone—not just someone, but his fated mate—sent a joyous sense of awkward and eager terror through his very bones. That stress found promise in his hands and legs, and he fought to control the trembling.

He...was trembling because he suddenly knew exactly what he wanted. But was it something Lune would want, too?

"You cheated again," Lune said with a lazy languidness, his arms raised above his head. "Using your magic to dress yourself."

Lune was so close, yet Narsus didn't know how to begin. This was all so foreign to him, no matter how much he secretly desired such comfort and intimacy. He had to clear his throat. "Next time, I'll try to remember not to use spells."

That put a delighted smile on his Intended's full lips. "I look forward to it."

Narsus couldn't stop staring at that mouth. Pale, as if bleached from the sun. Not too sun-baked, but not overly hydrated either. That mouth was the threshold of their future together. "What would you like me to do?"

"I want you to get used to touching me," Lune said. "I don't mind what you do. Bring us off, if that's what you desire."

Narsus wanted so much more than that. He didn't know why he had to work to pull the words out of his mouth. No. That was a lie. It was because no matter how far they'd come, he still couldn't get over the fear of his poison.

The truth was his deepest, truest desire. He wanted to be with this loving, caring siren for the rest of his days. It renewed his courage to ask the question. "Lune? May...may I kiss you? It would have to be through the scarf, though. For your own safety."

Lune's eyes went wide. That mouth wiggled with candid, elated glee. Fascinated, Narsus watched those plump lips flex and purse. But it was several seconds before he got an answer.

"Are you ready for that intimate a pledge and commitment?" Lune asked with hushed affection. "Are you sure?"

"Wholeheartedly, my songbird."

Lune tilted his chin up and his beautiful brown eyes sparkled. "Oh, I do favor that endearment."

Narsus caressed that jaw, savoring the touch through his gloves. "A normal marriage and a Compass-match are the same. The only difference is the fated mate match helps fuel the gestalt magic used by priests and Elementals.

"Lune, I want us to be us. A something wonderful that exists in concert alongside our Compass-bond. And outside it—most especially outside it. I wish for a union that is just us. Not one created just because of fated mate magic."

Narsus closed his eyes, leaning into the caress Lune gifted to him through the linen scarf mask.

"Your marriage proposal brings me so much pleasure, and I accept. Eagerly." Lune ran fingertips down the heavy wool of his tunic. "Have you ever kissed before, my Narsus?"

He shook his head.

Lune took a gentle inhale. "May I lead the kiss that weds us?"

Narsus let the small laugh rumble from the depths of his chest. "You sound so sure of yourself, orchestrating our kiss. Have you been wed before?"

Lune's guffaw vibrated through Narsus to the very core. "No, my phoenix. But we'd all sneak behind the schoolhouse when the adults weren't watching. It was intercourse mostly. Sometimes we dared to practice kissing. We were more scared of getting caught kissing than having our pants down."

"What schoolboys didn't panic about that?" Narsus said faintly.

Lune's expression morphed to melancholy. "I'm sorry. I can't even begin to fathom how lonely you were."

It took a moment before Narsus could find his voice. "Lonely no longer. Were you ever caught?" He traced a gloved finger slowly along Lune's jaw, intoxicated by the intimacy when Lune turned into his touch.

Embarrassment highlighted the curve of Lune's cheeks. "Cal figured it out at some point. He looked the other way as long as our, er, uh, *extended* fun didn't include anyone who was equipped to conceive. He actually had that very frank conversation with me. He also told me to tell the others we better stop kissing or else he'd report that behavior to our parents."

It was Narsus's turn to snort, adding a hearty laugh to the fun. "I *can't even* picture Cal telling you and everyone else to keep your lips to yourselves!"

It was right in the middle of that mirth Lune reared up and their mouths met. Narsus froze and stopped breathing at that point, causing Lune to withdraw.

"I didn't mean to—"

"Didn't want to exhale my poison into you," Narsus rushed to cut him off, readjusting the layers of fabric. "The scarf doesn't work like that—at least not in that type of contact. I'd dearly love to try again."

Lune's concern washed away. "Ready?"

Narsus quietly inhaled enough to sustain himself. "Ready," he agreed in a low, eager tone.

The scarf between them was thick, and scratchy enough that Narsus winced. The material stretched tight across his nose and mouth, tasting of burnt cotton and his own sweat.

Maybe this hadn't been a good idea after all. He'd just wrecked this pivotal, special moment. Why couldn't he have waited until they dealt with a way to neutralize his poison?

But with Lune's slow guidance, the gentle twists and rubs of his siren's plump lips pressed through the fabric, and rescued the experience of their first kiss as true mates. *As husbands.*

Narsus's shoulders relaxed, welcoming the sweeping caresses of Lune's touches. He had no idea his small moan escaped; the sound of it was absorbed into the barrier between them.

Without missing a beat, Lune's lips parted just a little wider, welcoming that moan inside. The intimacy of it sent raging warmth into Narsus's belly. Lune further distracted him by collecting the tail of his scarf. Using it as additional reassurance to cradle his cheek. Narsus leaned into it for a moment, then slowly moved back from the kiss, drawing in deep, but gentle gasps.

"Too much?" Lune asked, also breathless.

"N-no, it was so very much enjoyable." Narsus pulled the scarf to sit back on the bridge of his nose. "I'll always recall our first. It has a permanent place forged into my heart. But I'm going to have to work hard to find a way for our second to be skin-to-skin."

Lune's fingers dug into Narsus's shoulder. "I wouldn't trade that kiss for anything, my husband. Thank you for trusting me, and especially yourself enough for it."

Brows bent, Narsus glanced away, unable to steady his pounding heart. Pleased at the praise as well as Lune's trust, but a little embarrassed by it. He adjusted the fit of his gloves for something to do. Soft rustling drew his attention back.

Lune pointed to the mask left in the sand.

The mask? Narsus leaned over to retrieve it, turning it around and around as he fidgeted with it.

Lune's quiet suggestion caressed his ears. "An additional boost of courage plus a safeguard for you, while spicing things up between us."

Yes. The mask would do just that. Narsus put it on.

Lune nestled back into the sand. Arms and legs splayed. "Now," Lune coaxed gently. "Let yourself explore."

Narsus hesitated.

Lune merely turned over and presented his back. Face resting on his folded arms. "Is this easier?"

Breath ragged, Narsus choked out a yes. He settled himself half on Lune's butt, and half on his own knees. Loving the press of their parts.

"Mmmm," Lune mumbled dreamily. "That feels nice. I love the weight, the heat of you."

Narsus *was* burning a little hotter than usual. In one place in particular. He leaned over, playing with the golden strands of wavy hair draped over Lune's neck and around his shoulders.

"Like tassels of corn silk," he said aloud. Although Narsus wished he could experience the texture first hand, and not through the thick barrier of gloves. The fit of his trousers got even more snug.

Lune responded to him by lifting that round, solid ass. Up, down, up, and down. The slow, controlled undulations, followed by his husband's long, panting moans, made Narsus growl. The slight itching pressure in his mouth started up again as his fangs began to advance. His grunt must have highlighted his panic.

"I've seen them," came Lune's throaty and soothing voice. "When you get nervous or excited. Even when you try to hide them. They excite me too. Let them come, if you want. I won't look for now. Only when you want me to."

Lune was telling the truth. His siren's heart was beating fast, even as that ass rose again to push into his crotch. Narsus's tongue curled around his lengthening incisors. The blood pills were working, keeping the frenzied need to bite in check. His fangs weren't the only thing on him expanding, but it wasn't time for that. Now was learning to touch. To feel. To connect with his new husband on a level other than carnal, penetrative sex—which he still wasn't sure if they could even do.

One thing at a time. Just breathe.

Narsus exhaled and relaxed. Stroking his gloved hands along the length of Lune's clothed back. Firm flesh and solid muscle from his siren's years at the ocean-side. The narrow angles of Lune's waist. The flat of his back that dipped before gently sloping upwards to meet the roundness of his ass. He knew the skin to be kissed by the sun. Narsus was suddenly so very envious of the sun.

Inch by inch, Narsus's gloved hands made their way back up, lingering upon the bowed, quivering shoulders. Sweeping a lover's caress along that arched neck. Stroking, exploring. Cupping that cheek when Lune turned his face against his hand.

It was so tempting, so erotic to want to shove his fingers in that questing, yearning mouth, but Narsus dare not with the cloth gloves he currently wore. He filed that hope and desire away for another day. Even as he watched Lune's tongue chase his fingers after a stroke, a pat, or a lingering grope that had withdrawn to seek another conquest.

Lune's ass rose again, nestling into Narsus's pelvis. Narsus found himself offering the same pressure in return.

His phoenix body heat was beginning to take its toll on Lune as well. His siren's hair clumped in damp tendrils, plastered against that sun-tanned neck. As was the perspiration starting to dot in patches around his siren's clothing. The longer they played, the more dangerous sweat sodden linens might transmit his poisons. He had to finish this.

"Lune?" His words were strangled. "You're sweating too much. We should stop."

"I want to finish this." Lune's voice was heavy, panting. "Please."

"Then.. may...may I grind against you? May I come?"

Lune turned his head. "May I watch, and participate? I really want to wrap my legs around you."

Narsus moved so Lune could rearrange himself on his back. They settled against each other with such ease, Narsus felt the urgent stress to rub and rock pour into every inch of his being. The pressing weight of Lune's thighs wrapped around his ass, those heels pressing into his buttocks. This was meant to be.

Hands clasped against Lune's and squeezing, they now faced each other. Narsus bent forward. Lune's sweaty, moaning face was side-by-side with his stoic leather mask, barely touching. Inside his mask, Narsus too, was sweaty, moaning. He wanted to be close, so he put his trust in the mask. To keep his husband safe from his poisonous breath.

Intermittent huffs in the confined space of his mask fogged the lenses. But with each inhale, the lenses cleared. Giving him precious seconds to absorb the peaking joy beaming across Lune's flushed features, watching, silently begging for more.

"NnnnNar? Are you okay with this? Being this close to me?"

The heat and static swimming in Narsus's brain made hiding within the mask more intimate. "I like touching you. The mask doesn't put you off?"

Lune shook his head, candidly showing his joy at the weight atop him. Purring, groaning, savoring the heat of their wiggles and grinds. Lune let his fingers glide along the smooth black leather. Tracing the grooves of the tiny filigree designs.

"The mask lends you a sense of safety," Lune managed between moans and huffs for breath. "Enough to keep being close to me. Why should I fear that? It provides you the freedom of expression—your touch against me is gentle but eager."

When Lune nuzzled the mask, Narsus was lost. Moreso when Lune's tongue flicked out along the tip of the leather beak.

He came, and Lune came with him.

Narsus lost all strength in his shaking limbs. He braced his arms flush against the sand, and bent his head as he tried to catch his breath. His masked face resting briefly against Lune's shoulder. He did his best to keep most of his weight off Lune's body, and thus keeping their sweat from further mingling.

As their heaving slowed, Narsus realized Lune was reaching for the cloak. Narsus pulled it close. Unsure why he wanted it, but giving it to him. Lune tucked the excess between their bodies as a barrier, flipping the remainder over Narsus's back.

Narsus understood and assisted in the task. When it was done, his siren hugged him. He squeezed his eyes shut, and the welcomed sensation by leaning into it. Another hug. Lune's hug.

His heart soared as if it had wings of its own.

Chapter 17

NARSUS'S KISS HAD BEEN barely leashed banked fire. An inferno Lune gladly fell into. It had tasted of damp, smoky, scorched cotton. And tenderness. The texture of the cloth rubbing against his lips had gripped his gut, and his dick. It was a gift Lune would always treasure.

By the cracking of dawn, they stumbled back to their room. The enclosed suite still smelled a bit smoky, and the bed linens of sweat. Lune pursed his lips and his nostrils flared, enjoying the smell. Light char dusted the bedding and unblemished walls. He had a strange desire to roll in it, but voicing it had Narsus shaking his head, for he was still concerned about toxins and poisons. Instead, he helped Narsus do a quick tidy of their room.

Bathed and fully dressed, they both lay back on the clean sheets of the bed to rest and recover. They were propped up on their respective pillows and reclining against the headboard. They listened in companionable quiet to the ebb and flow of the lulling ocean waves against the sand. Watching the sunrise through the massive circular window. Trying to unwind from the dramas of the evening.

Lune toyed lovingly with the length of his compass chain. Narsus held his sea shell, turning it this way and that. Angling its polished surface to catch the glow of the morning rays.

Lune shivered lightly because another jewel had winked out while they'd been at play. Making it the ominous day number nine. It was time to break the lulling good-will between them. Because Lune knew whatever the darken jewels meant, wasn't a good thing.

"Narsus, it's time to tell me. What happens if all the jewels stop shining? Why is it so important?"

His husband seemed to place deeper attention upon his wedding gift. "It's a timer. To cement the bond-magic. Thirteen jewels, thirteen days before both compasses will go dark and reset."

"Reset?"

Narsus nodded. "Usually it's not an issue, as during the ceremony, the compasses are touched to the marriage stone, then to each other in order to fully sync up. I never gave us the chance to do that."

Lune placed a hand to Narsus's chest. "Please stop beating yourself up over this. We'll get through it."

Narsus sighed. "I'll try. But I won't fully forgive myself until the ceremony is complete."

"So what happens if the jewels burn out before we can sync the compasses? Does the magic that makes us compatible just stop?"

Narsus left their bed, and Lune's heart sunk. Was what he had to say so horrible? Quietly, Lune got up and followed a respectful distance behind.

·♥·♥·♥·♥·♥·

The question upset Narsus so much that he got up, and as calmly as he could, moved to the window. He pressed his forehead against the cool pane and just stood there. He was grateful when Lune followed, hovering, but not close enough to touch.

"If the compasses aren't synced up by the thirteenth day," Narsus said tightly. "Our Compass-pairing's lost. Our connection is lost. The compasses revert back to magical seeds and return to our bodies."

"And the magic will search out a new pairing?" Lune guessed slowly. "With someone else?"

"Yes."

"Oooohh!" Lune's controlled, even tone that was more like a growl said it all. Narsus dare not turn to look at his husband. "Verdigris be damned!"

"I'm already damned," Narsus agreed simply. "And undead."

Lune loomed too close. Narsus flinched and stepped back. Thankfully, Lune did not further crowd him.

"This isn't about your poisons, or your vampiric or demi-god status," Lune said. "Don't think bringing up those particular parentages will deter me from being angry. I should give you a good swift kick in that Compass-birthmark of yours."

Lune crossed his arms and leaned against the wall. He wasn't yelling. Narsus didn't know if that was worse.

"I *do* understand *why* you closed yourself off," Lune went on. "I do thank you for being so vulnerable and trusting with me. But how *dare* you make the decision to keep me in the dark."

Narsus accepted the scolding. They had kind of talked about it, previously, but never really got into Compass-lore deadlines. But now that they knew they could use Lune's compass to track his, a lot of the stress was draining away. Not all of it, but most. He beheld his husband from the corner of his eye. Lune was standing straight up now. Arms still crossed, but foot tapping. This vision made him bust out laughing.

Lune's eyebrows shot up and he wheezed out, "You find our Compass-separation funny?"

"What I find funny is that oh-so-familiar expression on your face. And the way you're standing. Soooo proper! Oh, gods, it's so Calico." Narsus doubled over, holding his middle as he laughed at Lune's offended reaction. "Oh, that scowl, too!"

This time Lune was fighting against a smirk. "I suppose being mad is a waste of energy. And seeing you laugh. So freely. Narsus..."

Calming himself, it took Narsus a moment longer for the mirth to subside. "I apologize with my entire heart, my Compass-mate. Know that I am working hard to make up for my mistakes."

"I know," Lune said softly, looking out into the dawn blushing against the horizon. "So let's get to searching, shall we?"

"Oh, do I finally get to see your Jade Raptor?" Narsus asked eagerly.

"No. Sachin has her out on hire. Not sure when he's coming back."

"Then how—?"

Lune only grinned. With easy, flittering movements of his fingers, he motioned to Narsus's arms. "You're going to carry me."

"*W-what?*"

"We're flying, my Narsus. By phoenix express since the sun's up. It's the fastest way and we have *a lot* of work to do."

Narsus was still unwilling to test Lune's possible immunity to his poison. So he'd frantically dug through storage closets in search of thicker clothing for Lune to wear. Lune assured him Calico had taken most of his clothing with him, and that he wouldn't find the capes and long-sleeved garments he was looking for.

The Star Land Islands were forever warm to serve phoenix-kind. There wasn't a need for most people to own or even wear winter clothing—unless one decided to venture into the inner forests and mountains.

When Narsus grumbled at the useless search, Cinder handed his sturdy coat-cape with its hood and decorative tails to Lune. The Cottage phoenix then retreated back to his shared quarters with Brightside without a word. Before the orange phoenix closed the door, Brightside called out not to mind them, as they'd be heading back to the bookstore very soon to restock.

Narsus tensed when Cinder handed over the garment to Lune. Because Lune was just staring back at him, which made Narsus even more uneasy.

"You don't mind?" Lune finally asked when Cinder had gone.

"Let's not make this weird," Narsus replied honestly, then dropped his voice into a low whisper. "He was always a friend more than anything else. I was never in love with him. So no, it doesn't bother me. Because I'm trying to forgive myself. You've shown me I need to forgive myself. You've given me the courage for it."

Lune left the coat thrown over the chair before opening his arms. "Hug?"

Narsus walked into the embrace. Lingering, feeling the affection and love offered. Until he pulled back a little, and gave a gentle swat to the buttock that he suspected hosted the Compass-birthmark.

"Oh!" Lune jerked in his embrace and his eyes went wide. "Oh, my. Mmm. That was a delightful surprise."

Lune's startled giggle further melted his fears and doubts. "Time to go," Narsus said.

His siren grabbed the coat-cape. "Lead the way."

Chapter 18

DURING THE FLIGHT TOWARDS Staritti's Island, and Temple Prime, Lune found himself having to breathe shallow, and through his mouth. While clean, the intense, charred odors clinging to Cinder's garments made him choke and gag. The conflicting smells of garlic and roses permeated the fabrics. So he yanked the decorative sash from around his compass-belt to wrap around his nose and mouth. It also helped combat the wind at this altitude that was battering him head on.

Landing atop the cliffs before Temple Prime, Narsus shifted back into his humanesque self. "You took the ride well. I'm surprised."

Lune playfully scrunched up his nose and smirked. "Calico, remember? Free rides."

"Ah, yeah, right."

"You sound disappointed."

"I was hoping to get that gloating honor." Narsus hunched his shoulders and kicked at the small rocks around the cliff-side.

"You're...actually pouting!" Lune's jaw dropped, but was more of a grin. "You have the rest of our lives to fly me around." Lune reached up, then paused, waiting for the permission to lay a gloved hand to Narsus's cheek.

Narsus took it, pressing Lune's touch lightly to his face. They shared a moment of an easy smile.

"Time to get to work," Lune reminded softly, letting go. He took off all his clothes and stuffed them into the pack. "Give me two days, at least, to make some wide sweeps before I start narrowing the search and circling inward. Or further outward. Temple'll feed you, yes?"

"Yeah, I'll be fine. Family will be sure I eat, and my childhood room's still open to me in the Grim's apartment suite. What about you?"

Lune made a face. "Fish or whatever. When I'm ready for pickup, I'll perch myself on..." He looked out into the ocean. "That rock. There."

Narsus noted the pickup point. "Understood. Good luck, Lune."

"Our luck's right here." He motioned to the compass bound around his wrist.

Narsus shifted back into his phoenix form and bunched his cape up within his talons to use it like a rope. He took flight, hovering in place. Lune reached out to grip the thick fabric.

"All set," Lune called.

Narsus rose higher and flew back over the ocean. That was when Lune let go and dove into the waves.

Lune settled on the shallow bottom, waiting for the silt and sand he'd stirred up to settle. Lifting his compass out before him, he realized they probably should have done aerial mapping beforehand. Oh well, too late now.

Setting to work, Lune swam to the edge of the continental shelf. Where he startled and shook himself when he immediately got a signal. The compass spun rapidly, pointing out into the deeper realm.

Lune hesitated because of the ocean's ever-increasing pressure, then glided down the edge of the continental slope, and out across the abyssal plains.

Up and over underwater hills and mounts, then suddenly backtracking. Turning in more circles, before going deeper into a smattering of various trenches. Picking up quick meals from the aquatic flora and fauna as the hours rolled along.

It hit him suddenly. The pressure this far down squeezing at him. Lune's gills felt like they were on fire. So did his legs. Legs that he didn't seem to have any control over any more. He hadn't shifted.

This was the deepest he'd ever tried to go.

Hesitating, he checked his compass. He was so close. Nearly right on top of it. But he felt so sick. His sight blurred, and mild dizziness set in.

Disorientation this deep instantly filled him with dread. A bubble of tears and terror and thoughts of sharks speared through him. He froze, trying to collect himself and will away the dizziness.

There were still a few days left. There was time. It'd be okay. He'd surface. Confer with Narsus. Go home and get a good night's sleep and finish this in the morning. He knew he could push himself deeper into the trenches, but right now he was just too tired, stressed, and worn out.

So he turned and kicked towards the surface. Doing so eased the weight on his bones, and he started feeling better. His vision sharpened and the low pressure headache vanished. Yes. Much better. It'd be okay. Nothing to worry Narsus over.

The wave of surface water nearly slammed Lune into the perching rock. He lost his grip and had to wait for the next ebb and flow. He held on with the second try. Narsus was there, waiting, and brought him back to the cliff-side the same way he'd been dropped off.

"Any luck?" Narsus transformed back into his human-self.

Lune was immediately wrapped in a large towel, and he clung to this lifeline. He struggled to take several breaths of the crisp air before he could even reply. "I—I was nearly right on top of it. But too tired right now."

"I can see that." Narsus engulfed him in a hug. Lune closed his eyes and savored it. "The weather's been pretty rough since I dropped you, and you were down so long I was starting to worry. We'll find it tomorrow," Narsus reassured. "We have time. You need to rest, and I want to take you home."

Home sounded wonderful. Home with Narsus.

Chapter 19

ONCE BACK IN THEIR room, Lune flopped on the bed and glanced down to the luggage left at the footboard. "I've been meaning to ask. What's in this big rucksack you've never opened?"

"Extra clothes. Gloves. My emergency medical kit. ...Other stuff."

"Oh, other stuff like blood pills? What?" Lune asked at the stunned expression on his husband's face. "Come on, really? You wouldn't think I'd know? Just because we're on a sunny island chain doesn't mean vampires are excluded from the school curriculum. If you really want to get into gritty details, remember the Grim's my adopted brother, even though I've only seen him from a distance. Mostly at the festivals. He actually waved to me, once. And if it wasn't for the birthday money he'd send me every year, I'd still be saving up to buy my boat."

"Yyyeah...Dad doesn't do well among the living. He inherited too much of Grandpa Cal's space-time abilities, which can make him moody and quiet. He can be quite fun though, and certainly has a sense of humor. Thankfully, I inherited only the undead bits. I have enough to deal with from my phoenix heritage."

"So, what else is in your med kit?" Lune turned down the blanket on his side of the bed.

"Uh. Um." Narsus fiddled with the luggage closures before finally opening the pockets. "A supply of activated charcoal. It's also ingestible if someone happens to get too close. It helps extract the oils and poisons and such from one's system."

Lune stopped. And stared. "And why didn't you tell me about this before?"

"It's for emergencies only."

"Our initial meeting didn't constitute as an emergency?" Lune huffed. "Don't you think we could've used this so much earlier?"

Narsus winced and said nothing

"We're fated mates," Lune reminded warmly. "Brought together by the magic of the compass. A compass that we're retrieving tomorrow, first thing when the sun rises. But for now, break out the charcoal and take off that cloak and hat. It's time to relax for the night and play."

The activated charcoal came in two forms. Powder and paste. Lune chose the paste first. He dipped his pinky within the jar, then lifted it to his lips. And spread it along the contour of his mouth.

Narsus gulped. Licking his own lips. Feeling the heat rising in his dick.

Lune tormented him further when he took a paintbrush from the drawer and lightly dabbed it into the powder. Tapping the brush against the rim, he turned briefly to look in the mirror of the vanity dresser.

Narsus watched as Lune dusted the brush bristles gently against the highest part of his cheekbones. When that was done, he once again sought the paste. With two fingers now, he closed his eyes and smeared the paste upon his eyelids. The black against Lune's rich, brown eyes was a sight that struck him right in the gut.

Narsus breathed. "That's a serious creative turn-on."

"We both know you're not yet ready for that."

"Where did you learn to—"

Lune laughed, holding the noise inside. "Isolated islands have courtesans too, silly city boy. Don't tell Cal what I did with my hoarded birthday money."

"You bet I won't. What did you have in mind for this?"

"How about a replay of our marriage kiss? You wanted it skin-to-skin?" Lune merely dipped two bare fingers back into the paste, then slowly lifted them toward Narsus's uncovered mouth. Narsus reared back.

"Too soon?" Lune asked softly.

"Too soon," Narsus mumbled, looking away.

"That's all right." Obediently, Lune brushed the excess back into the jar. "Then how about I just hug you? With wandering hands?"

"That...could work. As long as you don't touch my face or hair." Narsus wrapped up his braid in a long veil pulled from his luggage.

He reached for the beaked mask and slipped it on.

"It would be more intimate without it." Lune offered the scarf that usually covered his nose and mouth instead. "I promise I won't go any higher than your shoulders. And I'll wear gloves."

Narsus watched Lune pull a pair into view and put them on. They were long gloves, ones that reached up to his elbows. For added measure, Lune also rolled down the sleeves of his blouse, and buttoned up the area that showed off the sculpted angles and planes of his smooth chest.

"The mask is a lovely and exciting kink, my cockerel phoenix. But do you want to try without it this time?"

His elevated breath fogged up the mask's lenses. Fists clenched, Narsus agreed with a curt nod, but he was scared. Slowly, he pushed the conical beak upward, revealing his face. They stared at each other for a few moments, and he liked the way Lune's soft brown gaze traveled across his features. Licking his lips, Narsus pushed the mask all the way off.

"Maybe," Lune suggested. "When you finally construct your own, it'll make for some intense play."

Narsus was suddenly calculating how long it would take him to decide on a design and finish the damn thing. "I like that idea," he managed. "A lot."

"May I?" Lune lifted his hands.

Tense but eagerly agreeable, Narsus stepped into Lune's personal space.

Lune's gloves were torturous joy. The pressure of the slow, questing touch was exhilarating, nerve-wracking. The sensations zipping into his gut.

Narsus wanted it to stop, yet continue forever. It overwhelmed him. Over-stimulated him to the point where he wanted to turn and sink his teeth into Lune's shoulder. But that too, scared him. He didn't know just how much of his father's cursed heritage was within him. But gods...how he wanted to bite. *So badly.* He must have made a noise for the hands paused, then lifted away.

"Too much?"

Narsus could only pant. He wanted to answer, but he was shaking. He tried to answer. He could only grunt, gasp. Think about his teeth toying with his mate's flesh.

"Shhhh," Lune soothed.

Narsus panicked. Lune was moving away. Narsus seized his husband's hand, pulling him back. Clutching that gloved hand against his chest. To where his heart was beating so wildly. Narsus could feel the blood pumping through his undead veins. Hear it whoosh in his ears. And with Lune this close, Narsus could hear his mate's, too. Sense it. Smell it. Feel it. Lune's heart. Lune's blood.

"Come lay down on your side," Lune offered.

Narsus obeyed. The blankets were tangled and twisted. Bunching up beneath him in all the right places. Sensitive places. Oh gods. What was Lune doing to him?

He had to bite. Was going to. The urge, growing. The instinct awakening. He should stop. Take his pills. But it was too late.

Crazed, panicked, Narsus did the only thing he could. He seized the edge of his pillow and shoved it into his mouth. Trying to ease the pounding, raging need. The desire. Biting down. Hard. The fabric filling his mouth was an undead godsend. He only wished it was flesh. Lune's flesh, and his blood. Warmed by the sun and smelling of the ocean. But he had to make do.

Lune's scent. Thoughts of the hot sand when he revealed his true, elemental form. Salt and seaweed. All driving him wild. Suck. And mate. His hips jerked once, then he froze. What was he doing?

"Gods," Lune's throaty whisper broke the trance. "So beautiful. Keep going."

Lune's hands kept going, too. Cupping Narsus's ass with wide, firm strokes.

Narsus squeezed his eyes shut and gave in. Future condemnation and embarrassment be damned. Up and down in a frenzy, his slim hips rode the bunched-up sheets beneath him. His jaw clenched further, his teeth ripping the fabric. His eyes began to water. He was so close to coming, wanted to come. But these sensations weren't enough. His distress must have shown.

"Would this help?" Lune asked softly, climbing into bed with him.

His siren guided him up on his hands and knees. Then knelt behind him, his hard dick poking, pressing snugly against Narsus's ass. Gently, but deliberately grinding into the seat of his trousers.

Narsus's eyes rolled back, and he tried to breathe. Lune's loving touch, stroking him, rubbing his balls through the layers of clothing. With a guttural moan, Narsus spent himself in his trousers and collapsed to the mattress.

A cloak fluttered atop Narsus before Lune rested his weight flush against his back. When the ringing in Narsus's ears began to fade, he realized he was still breathing heavily. Pulling the pillow out of his mouth and off his receding fangs. He spit out the trailing fibers.

"Vampire phoenix?" Lune asked with breathy affection, looking at the twin punctures on the pillow. "I had no idea an averted bite could turn me on. We may have to explore the real thing sometime."

Surprised at feeling the blush rise in his face, Narsus pursed his lips. To give himself time to think about how to respond. "As you know, I...don't require blood to survive—lucky, I guess. A few of my siblings do. But since it is a big part of my heritage, I sometimes fall to the desires. In the last few days, though, I feel a...pressing thirst. Maybe it has to do with age. Or deep emotion. Dad always said to take it slow. I'm thankful for the blood pills now."

"How much of you is undead?"

It was difficult to talk about this. He didn't want to, but Lune had a right to know. After all, Lune had freely shared his own history. "My egg was found to be non-viable after it was laid. I would've just been buried and forgotten forever, but the Compass-mark was glowing on my shell. I was brought to Temple Prime and offered up to the Grim. To keep the Compass-magic going.

"The Grim became my father, my mentor. I love him. He loves me. He's treated me well. We have strong father-son bonds. But sometimes, living among the undead...being one of them...can be...grotesque and traumatic. And well, we just don't know all about what's going on with me yet. I guess."

Narsus welcomed the gloved hand that reached out for him. He allowed it to linger and comfort.

"We'll face whatever manifests," Lune vowed.

Their quiet moment was precious, but Narsus sensed there was something unfinished between them. A mild frustration that wasn't his lost compass. So when Lune slowly, deliberately, pursed his mouth, Narsus's attention was once again lured to his mate's charcoal-painted lips.

Lune knew what Narsus was going to say before he said it.

"To kiss me is to court Death," Narsus reminded him softly, reluctantly drawing back from the embrace most cherished. "All of me is toxic. Poisonous. Even a quick peck to your cheek could make you gravely ill or cause blisters."

Lune didn't want to pressure Narsus, because it felt like he already was. But how to convince his husband to keep being brave without coming across as demanding and dominating? Because an actual kiss was the one last thing that kept them apart. Well, that and still needing to find the compass.

Through their bedroom window, Lune looked out onto the starry horizon. Staring at Narsus now would just enforce the idea that his fears didn't matter. "We already know I'm immune to your fire. And to the poison—somewhat. I'm willing to take that risk."

"Are you?" Narsus's voice was so stressed and hoarse, that Lune had to catch his breath. "What if I'm not willing?" Narsus went on. "I wonder if you're—just how much damage you're hiding from me. Hurting you would destroy me."

"Why?" Lune asked, eyes watering. In a thready whisper, he asked again, "Why would it destroy you, Narsus?"

"Because I think I love you."

Those words. Words he didn't realize he'd been waiting to hear. Lune squeezed his eyes shut. His gulping breaths struggled for stability.

Narsus had braced himself against the bed. Obviously waiting in an anxious limbo for a response.

Lune opened his eyes, arms outstretched. "I think I love you right back."

Narsus rushed forward, a small cry on his lips. Lune's arms came around him and held tight, knowing his mate needed this. So badly. He did, too.

Lune rubbed at Narsus's trembling back through the heavy layers of clothing. "I so want to pull off that veil. Run my fingers through your hair," Lune said. "But you know I won't. Is it as soft as it looks?"

"Probably." Narsus answered. "By the gods, I want to taste that mouth of yours. But I won't."

"Maybe you *should* taste me." Lune smiled. "I dare you."

Again, with gloved hands, Narsus traced the curve of Lune's painted lips.

"Kiss me," urged Lune's soft whisper. "Please. With naked lips. Like we both've been wanting. Make this a real, official marriage. Not just one built on holding back and 'I thinks.' Narsus? I lied when I said I think I love you. I *know* I love you." To prove his declaration, Lune pulled the charcoal canister out of the rucksack and held it out to him. "Do you *love* me? Just to clarify—love, and being in love are two separate feelings. Both are valid. Although I know the latter takes more time. I'm very willing to be patient, and ecstatic for either one."

Against his better judgement, Narsus tilted his head, and his eyes bobbed. The smattering of freckles across Lune's sun-tanned face were fascinating to behold. Lune enticed him further, moistening those plump lips. When that tongue peaked out to do the deed a second time, Narsus was lost.

His shuttering cry escaped before his words could. "I do. I do love you, Lune."

Lune gave a happy little cry before he eagerly reapplied the charcoal to his lips. And as if to torment him further, Lune took his time to tease. To pucker. Show off a bit of tongue.

Their mouths met in a timid brush. Narsus pulled back to scan for blemishes that were not there. Embolden, he returned for more. It was a dance of lips that turned into a long, flowing waltz. Narsus gasped for breath with each small intermission, even as he was desperate for more.

Losing control, he rubbed his lips across Lune's cheek.

Their arms pressed tighter. Their hands roamed faster.

Until Narsus saw it. A bright red rash quickly spreading across Lune's skin where he had peppered his kisses. Horrified, Narsus yanked away.

"What?" Lune asked. "What's—wrong?" In that second, Narsus knew Lune felt it, for his siren touched his purpling mouth, probing at the damage. The blistering spread before Narsus's eyes, cracking those soft, perfect lips. Discoloring the sun-tanned skin into a purplish-green bruise. The charcoal had done nothing.

Lune's eyes rolled back into his head and he lost consciousness.

"NOOooooo! Lune! Lune!" Narsus caught him as he fell to the floor. *"By the gods, what have I done?"*

The door flew open. Brightside and Cinder stood within, backlit by the hall light.

"Help me," Narsus cried.

Brightside shot forward and helped usher Lune to the rumpled bed. Terror sluiced along Narsus's veins. His husband was so limp and pale, and the poison was spreading, even to where they hadn't touched. Lune's eyelids and mouth were going puffy and pink.

"I'll get the activated charcoal," Cinder said, already digging through the bag on the floor.

Narsus sat on his side of the mattress, head bowed. Pulling his cowl over his head to keep from doing any more harm. He didn't even realize Cinder stood over him until his friend jostled him with a bump. "Nar, look."

He couldn't. It was difficult enough to accept that he had done this. He'd harmed the one person who believed in him. Trusted him, loved him enough to be vulnerable.

The hand yanking on his cowl forced him out of his despair.

"Look at his face," Cinder demanded.

He didn't want to.

"Look at him, Nar," Brightside repeated. "He's healing. Incredible. I haven't even applied additional charcoal yet."

Narsus gasped. Lune's eyes were open. The swelling had lessened, but hadn't faded entirely. Where the lips had been split and bleeding, it was now dried and crusted over. But strangely, where the poison had sat, the faint texture of scales surfaced. Narsus wanted to touch that, to see if his eyes were deceiving him. Perhaps it was just his anxiety and guilt playing tricks. But he dare not chance another touch. Another kiss. Not ever again.

"Nar..." Lune rasped, reaching out to him, his eyes opening but unseeing. "Don't blame."

Lune's grip went slack, and the hand fell. Those eyes slowly closed as his siren fell back into unconsciousness.

Chapter 20

NARSUS STAYED AT LUNE's bedside. Apologized a million times. Poured out his heart. Nothing had helped.

The damage of his misguided and regretful kisses was nearly gone. But it had been nearly the entire day. Narsus didn't know if Lune was just healing, or in a coma. So he paced.

"You're going to wear a hole into Calico's throw rug. Narsus, he's okay." Brightside sat calmly in a chair dragged from the parlor and into the master bedroom. Arms crossed, the elf's expression was one of no nonsense. "I checked him over. The town healer checked him over. Lune's not in distress, and he's breathing fine. Give him time."

"But the scales," Narsus protested.

Brightside shrugged. "His kind are probably resistant to certain poisons. Especially given there are many sea creatures poisonous themselves."

"But the scales," Narsus repeated anxiously.

"He *is* a siren," Brightside reminded. "Did you think that maybe your poisons woke up his shape-shifting abilities? Maybe as a defense? Because only the flesh of his human-self reacted badly. There's no affliction to his scales."

"What's wrong with my scales?"

Narsus whipped around and knelt at the bedside.

"Oh," Lune exclaimed. "They're thicker than my previous shift. Wow. Neat." He was picking and poking at his partially shifted arms. "Nar, look, I can shift. Like you."

Narsus flinched when Lune reached out to him. "Please, don't touch me."

"What? Why?" Lune asked, pulling back to examine himself again. He ran fingertips across the overlapping yet neatly patterned scales. "It's not slimy. Huh. I wonder if siren scales have a slime coat. Maybe it activates when I get back into the water for the first time with them." He glanced down. "Oh! Webbed hands now? Oh, wow. I can't wait to try these out in the water. I wonder how far I can shift."

When Lune said that, the webbed membrane between his fingers folded out of sight. "Oooooh," Lune exclaimed. "I wonder..." The flaps then snapped back into existence as thick, scaly plates between the digits. Complete with claws.

"I'll excuse myself now." Brightside closed the door behind him to grant them privacy.

"Do you think you're strong enough to get out of bed?" Narsus was surprised he'd kept his voice from cracking at the turmoil.

His question broke Lune from his exploration. What transpired finally sunk in. "Oh," he said haltingly. "Narsus, I..."

Narsus clamped his teeth into his fist to keep from talking. Only motioned for Lune to stand up.

Lune moved to the edge of the mattress and tested his balance. "See? I'm fine."

Narsus collapsed into the chair Brightside vacated. Lune sat back on the bed and curled his bare feet against Narsus's boots.

"I-I can't think of anything other than your skin cracking and turning from my poison."

"Nar. I—I think it's like Brightside said. Your kisses made my siren-self appear, like before. I can't think of a nicer surprise. Because look. *Look at me, Nar.*"

Narsus lifted his gaze and could see only the arm Lune had nearly shoved in his face. There was a patch of fading, flaky red skin that ran right into a row of pristine metallic scales. On the other side of those scales was a continuation of that flaky red skin.

Narsus leaned back in the chair and ran his hands over his tearing eyes. "Your—Your siren form is immune to me?"

"Apparently so." Lune's fingers probed at his lips, assessing them. "While my human form seems to be trailing behind, but catching up. Lips are in full working order."

"Lune, thank the gods." Narsus heaved a breath as he fought a sob. "I'm so glad. But...but I—I need a moment to myself. Excuse me."

Narsus vacated his chair, but found himself halted by Lune's grip to his wrist. His husband clicked open his compass, confirming the number of jewels still lit. Raising it up to show him, as a silent warning. Then, "Narsus, my darling," Lune told him before letting go. "I understand. Take the time you need. I'll be here. Waiting for you. Then we'll go."

Day eleven.

Clicking the casing of his compass shut, Lune looked across the empty bed. He was starting to get antsy over the time constraint, but he felt confident today was the day. Everything would work out.

While disappointed, he knew he couldn't expect Narsus to just smile, and be happy now that all was well after centuries of inner turmoil. Emotions and trauma couldn't just be turned off like a switch. It had to age and process.

Dressed and heading out to the kitchen, Lune saw that Narsus had camped out on the living room floor. He smiled slightly when he saw the sea shell on a nearby table. It warmed him that Narsus didn't want to be parted from it. Leaving him to sleep, Lune decided to make breakfast.

He opened the pantry door and was surprised to see the beloved waffle iron on the shelf. As if it had never left. Taking advantage of the opportunity, he transferred it to the stove top to heat.

Growing up, Calico would always make waffles for him when he'd hit a crossroads, a problem with the other kids in the schoolhouse, or when he was feeling vulnerable and uncertain. Lune wanted to do the same for Narsus. But what could he substitute for the strawberry jam—when he turned, there were two baskets of fresh strawberries and a jar of pre-mixed batter already on the counter.

A gift basket via the God of Space and Time, and another note, telling him to keep his chin up. Lune shouldn't be startled, but he was, somewhat. Still, he knew Calico was always looking out for him.

"Thanks Dad, wherever you've gone," he said aloud, and with heart. "I needed this. Narsus does too. He just doesn't know it yet."

There wouldn't be time to make the jam itself. Butter would have to do. That was when Narsus slumped into the kitchen, further wrapped up in his mask, cape, hat, and gloves.

"Hungry?" Lune asked, pouring the batter into the hot mould.

That beaked mask muffled Narsus's grumpy snarl.

"Oh, my. The coffee's percolating for that mood. You could slice strawberries for me instead of standing there concealing that glower."

"I'm sorry," Narsus fidgeted with the mask. "I won't—"

"Won't what?" Lune interrupted gently. "Never kiss me again while I'm in human form? Because we both know that's just fear talking. Narsus, we're working all this out. See?" Lune pointed to the skin of his unblemished arms. "Scales have receded. Not even a scar. The

Compass-magic is letting me be close to you. My scales are letting you near. It's just taking time. Probably because we're still incomplete. The compass—"

"Maybe *I* still need to give it time."

"Our time to brood and cling to depression has run out." Lune pulled out his compass, pointing to the circle of gemstones. "Two days. We *will* find it. Today. We're so close. And yes, I'm feeling strong enough to go back this morning. That partial shift was like an entire pot of coffee. Coffee'll clear the cobwebs." He poured a cup and clanked it to the counter. "You're not a morning person, are you? Ah...I take that stiff body language as a no."

Lune turned back to the stove and peeled the waffle out of the iron mold. He dabbed a healthy amount of coconut oil onto the iron ridges and dumped in more batter.

"I don't hear you at the cutting board, slicing those strawberries," Lune said after a moment. "We need our strength because as I mentioned last night, we have a compass to reclaim."

Chapter 21

NOW AT THE CLIFF-SIDE, Lune knew for a fact today would be different. Soon they'd be official Compass-mates. Spending evenings curled up and cozy, resting together. In their bed. Listening to the comfort of the ocean waves.

His toes clutched at the rocks for balance. He gauged the winds, the currents, his distance. Then, naked, and with his compass securely bound to his wrist, Lune dove into the water. This was the first time he was back in his element since being poisoned. He waited, examining his limbs. Nothing changed. Maybe his body was still trying to adjust. He tread water a bit to get re-assimilated, then abandoned the expectation of a shape-shift.

Arm out in front of him, he used his compass as a beacon to bring him back to where he'd left off. He swam around in slow circles, narrowing down the pattern. Diving a bit lower at each turn.

But the deeper he went, something going on inside himself didn't feel right. His gills were flared open to full, but he wasn't getting much oxygen. His legs were tingling. Horrible pins and needles. It had to be the depths waking up his siren's body.

Suddenly, his compass glowed. Ecstatic, Lune worked to track and pinpoint his target. The deeper he went, the more stabbing and sharper his headache became. His vision started to blur. He was reaching his limit. Still, he pushed, telling himself he was almost there. He could do this.

His hands started to shake. The pressure was squeezing him.

There. *Narsus's compass.* He could see the round flatness of the metal against the grainy ocean floor.

He paddled downward and reached for it. But as he touched it, it was like a shot of lightning up his arm.

He froze in shock.

Beneath Narsus's compass, covered in barnacles and muck, was a...second compass?

Lune immediately grabbed both.

Using his fingernails and teeth on the second compass, he cracked the barnacles and scraped them off. The sweet and briny snack often sustained him when he submersed himself for hours to days. It was the one bit of sea edibles he could stand.

Yes, it was indeed a Compass, and he had a suspicion he knew who it belonged to. If Compass-borns tended to gather in groups, it made sense a lost compass could gravitate toward other compasses. Lune secured them both in the little drawstring carry bag he'd looped over his torso.

He turned to head back. Something inside him suddenly broke. Maybe he tried to ascend too fast. He couldn't breathe. He thrashed violently. His body was on fire from the inside out. The pins and needles in his legs went numb. His gills were flaring but not working. Or maybe overworked.

Lune gasped and thrashed again as liquid lava instantly seemed to attack his legs. His entire body spasmed, and he screamed. The pockets of air held in stasis in his lungs escaped him. Bubbles were bouncing up to the surface.

His legs. He couldn't move them. Felt as if they were turning into putty. He couldn't swim. He'd overestimated himself. Been too cocky by going so deep. Was...was he actually drowning?

Lune flailed, swallowing water that would not flow through his gills. His mind was fogging and his limbs grew heavy.

Narsus. Oh gods, Narsus. His mate would be devastated. It wasn't fair.

Chapter 22

THE SUN WAS SETTING. The fingers of darkness blended into the cast of the sun as if they were lovers. Being out here all day left Narsus with an odd feeling in his gut. Hadn't Lune said he'd known the general area? Shouldn't he have been back by now?

The pink sky was fading into pale purples and dark blues.

Generally, phoenix didn't like to fly at night. Or at least that's what Narsus learned growing up with the phoenix forges native to the archipelago. The solar rays of the sun aided their aerial mobility. Made their flight lighter, more efficient. And it did for him, too.

Although, the night had never been his adversary. He chalked it up to his undead bloodline. Narsus played within the realms of day and night with equal grace.

Had he already said it was getting late?

Narsus wasn't sure why he felt the urgency to be in the air. He should be circling over a specific stretch of water, but still he paced the cliff's edge. The wind was strangely calm this evening, and thus, not stirring up as many waves.

On guard, tense, and using the sharp night vision gifted to him by the Grim god, Narsus spotted the quick pop of air bubbles breaching the surface. It only lasted a few seconds, but in his heart he knew it was Lune.

In dire need of his help.

He dove off the cliffs in his phoenix form. Shifting into his more streamlined human-self just before hitting the ocean. Plowing straight down into the water.

Lune needed him. He needed Lune. Somewhere beneath these waves, his husband was panicking, unable to breathe.

And...and so was he.

Narsus knew he'd died, twice. Thrice.

At least five times that he was aware of.

Willingly, he traversed farther down into the depths. Permitting himself to be a puppet, one trapped between his phoenix blood and his vampiric blood. A dual heritage that now waltzed together within the murky gloom of the ocean deep.

Losing consciousness as his flames flared out. Only to jerk back into the realm of the living as the fiery green element flared brightly back into being. Only to have the cycles start all over again because he no longer had oxygen trapped in his lungs.

Despite being the child of the Grim, Narsus couldn't understand how he'd revived and continued to swim on without burning down to ash to be reborn. And especially without a chosen element to anchor his memories. Did this mean he was more undead than phoenix?

The wedding shell. His emotional attachment to it had become his grounding element that charged his rebirth. The gift filled the dark hole inside him where there'd previously been none to fuel him.

The surprise of this lightninged through his brain, but what was far more urgent to him was Lune. To find and reach his heart, his fated mate. His husband.

His sharp eyes found his target, even in the dark depths.

When he got to Lune floating so still, Narsus died yet again from grief.

The new shape of his mate only vaguely registered in his mind. But there wasn't time now. He had to get Lune back to the surface.

Wrapping an arm around that slim waist, he clawed his way upwards. Dying and reviving a handful more times before breaching the waves. Narsus shifted back into his phoenix body and took flight, with his talons locked around Lune's arms at the biceps.

Gently lowering him to the closest sandy beach. Once again in his human form, Narsus immediately sent up several fireballs to hover just feet above them. The light cast upon them, bright and clear.

Frantic, and not knowing what to do, he turned Lune on his stomach. Praying the water would drain from lungs meant for air. Praying that Lune's new form would figure it out—despite the shock it had just gone through. He didn't even know if doing this was the proper way to revive a siren in natural form. All Narsus knew was that Lune being in the water right now hadn't been a good thing.

There was a massive inhale and exhale that expelled a torrent of water—from Lune's mouth, and his gills. Lune flailed violently, and continued to gag and sputter, his beautiful dual tails thrashing. Narsus angled out of the line of fire, watching.

There wasn't any blistering or scarring across Lune's shoulders. Not even a nick from his talons when he'd carried him to safety. No hand-shaped outlines of poison where Narsus had turned him over to face the sand.

There was no damage.

Lune and Brightside were right. Lune was immune to him in siren form. Narsus let out a small snivel, holding his forehead to try and keep from breaking down.

There also was not a mark or scar or rip in those dual, and incredibly beautiful, marvelous fins!

Lune's strangled grunt drew his attention, and Narsus beheld the beautiful sight. Lune's chest was heaving, his lungs now drawing in that salty, precious air. His sopping wet blonde hair clung to his cheeks. The warm, sandy brown eyes were gone. Showcased in their place were slightly reflective, pale blue eyes against pale skin. Those eyes were squinting now. With a clawed, webbed hand raised to shield them from the brightness of his phoenix flame.

Narsus waved away all but one of the light-spheres and fell beside his mate. He gathered Lune up in his arms and held tight. His own body heaving at the elation and relief. His joyful cries renewed when Lune's arms came around him. Holding just as tightly.

When they parted, Lune's expression turned to one of concern. "You've changed," he rasped.

Lune's webbed fingers roamed over Narsus's face, toying with tracks of sodden little feathers at his hairline. Narsus reached up to explore them, too. He suspected his multitude of deaths would place stress on his body. Perhaps even merge his two forms together.

Taking mental stock of his new form, Narsus felt the heavy weight at his back. *Wings. He had wings in his human form, ready to lift him into the air at the mental beckon.*

He didn't care that he was no longer the same. All he wanted was Lune at his side. "We've both changed. You should see yourself," Narsus replied, lovingly caressing the fins that sprouted atop Lune's ears. The pearly and delicate translucent tips arched above the rounded helix, and shimmered from the water droplets. They looked very kissable, but that was an inquiry for another time.

Lune was busy staring down at the sand where his legs should be. The twin tails were coiled like snakes on each side of him. Balancing him and keeping him upright.

"Oh my," Lune marveled. "This is certainly different. I think...I think I like it. But how do I make them move? I seem to be having a little trouble."

"That's because your brain's gone through a bit of a change, too. Shifting is like a muscle, and you overworked it. Which is probably the cause of this scare. It'll take a bit to get used to. Give it a try."

Lune seemed to give it a go, but nothing happened. When he stuck out his tongue to concentrate, a limb twitched.

And they laughed, resting their foreheads together as their shaking fists clung upon the other for reassurance. Holding each other, within their cozy circle of phoenix light, recovering from all that had just happened.

Until Lune began to fuss with the bag over his torso.

"By the gods." Narsus spied the treasure in the netted carry-all. "Is that...my compass?"

"You can't tell? No, that's Brightside's."

Narsus's jaw dropped. "You found Bree's compass!"

Lune nodded, not bothering to hide his smirk. "But this one," he untangled them as he pulled them from the bag. "I know this belongs to you. Why is it in the ocean?"

When Narsus caught sight of the gleaming metal, he knew it belonged to him. He opened his mouth, having trouble answering. "I had a momentary lapse of judgment..."

"Yes," Lune agreed. "That's for certain. Aren't you going to say thank you?"

"Thank you," Narsus rushed. "Ah, gods, thank you for being here. For being you. And for being so patient and loving with someone so foolish, it takes them until now to realize how foolish they'd been."

"There's nothing to forgive, my phoenix."

Brushing the grime and sludge off his compass, Narsus opened the cover and got to his knees, humbling himself. He held it out for Lune to see. Two yellow jewels shone defiantly among their extinguished kin.

Seeing it, Narsus cleared out the bawl strangling his throat, and took a cleansing breath.

"Lune, will you join me as a Compass-mate? Holding hands? Laughing? Loving while we work to help sustain the magic we were born to curate? Will you forgive me for succumbing to my worst fears? Will you be my fated mate on this most beautiful eleventh day?"

"I will. So much yes, my Narsus. To it all."

Lune pulled his compass off his wrist. With shaking, unfamiliar clawed and webbed hands, he wrestled to open the cover. Touching the compasses together, the jewels flashed in unison, with all thirteen on both apparatuses lighting up.

There was a short cry of relief. From both of them. Releasing their pent-up fear over those shining lights.

The noise Lune made was an amalgam of a laugh and a full-blown cry. "Narsus, will you spend your days here, with me and the ocean?"

Narsus gathered Lune up in his arms and stood. "I would so very gladly stay with you. In your cozy and bright little beach house."

The wings sprang up from Narsus's back, and swept wide in their full glory. Lune's shocked gasp immediately turned into breathy admiration. He held on tighter. One tail coiled around Narsus's arm. The other tail anchored around Narsus's leg.

Narsus craned his neck to give himself a quick inspection. His wings were a striking array of greens with blue edging.

They looked at each other and laughed again. Easy humor that continued to draw them closer together, as fated mates should be.

"Let's go home."

"Yes," Narsus said as they launched into the dawn sky. "Let's."

Chapter 23

NARSUS BOUNCED UP THE steps to the beach house's front door. Folding his wings, he wasn't surprised when they disappeared. They were a gift to his human self. From the undead phoenix god. The appendages would return when he required them. Since he had his hands full, Lune pushed the door open, and they strolled in.

"We're home," Narsus called out. "Bree? Cinder?"

Silence.

"They must be out. Maybe back at that bookstore," Lune said.

"I don't see any note. Hungry?" Narsus set Lune down at the kitchen table.

Lune grabbed the table for balance as his new tails wrapped around the chair to further steady himself. "Savagely so. I have been since you plucked me out of the water."

"Shape-shifting takes a lot of energy." Narsus opened the pantry. "What do you want?"

"Waffles!" he shouted, laughing. Lune leaned over, trying to get a look at the shelves so recently stocked by Brightside and Cinder. "Waffles. Potatoes, and a steak the size of the beach house."

Narsus busted out laughing. "Steaks that big we'll have to go into town to get."

"Then waffles will have to do for the interim," Lune commanded. "It's time you learned how to make them—"

The front door suddenly slammed open. Brightside appeared in the kitchen archway, eyes wild, and his face ashen gray. Cinder hurried along right behind him, looking quite the same.

"Oh!" Lune cried, fumbling to unbind the compass he'd tied off on his wrist. "Brightside, look what we found!"

"I...I..." the elf stuttered. "Felt...it."

Brightside was nearly leaning into Lune now. And the elf only had eyes for the object Lune held out.

"It's here? You—you found it?" Brightside mumbled in awe, taking it. Cherishing it. "After all this time? Lune...thank you."

"And it's glowing. You're being called," Lune said.

"Yes...?" the elf whispered faintly, then looked at Narsus, as if lost.

Narsus smiled. "You should get going."

"Yes..." Brightside said again, still in a daze. He just stood there. Staring at his compass. Holding it as if he wasn't even sure what it was.

Until Cinder gave him an urgent nudge. *"Bree, let's go."*

Not even giving Lune's new siren body a second glance, the crow-like phoenix ushered Brightside into their room. Even with the door closed, there was the clatter of dresser drawers. Of Brightside's tearful, halting, and muffled conversation with an equally distressed Cinder.

"Well," Lune said, trying not to eavesdrop. He lifted his dual tails and wiggled them. "I'd love to try and walk on these noodles again. See how it works out."

Narsus shook his head. "This is your first real and complete shift. Get used to your new body and strengthen your muscles before you start getting creative. You don't want to hurt yourself. *Again,*" he added sternly.

Lune's eyebrows rose. "You speak from experience?"

He nodded. "I was a young hothead and tried to fly when I first transformed. I fell out of the sky from pretty high up—I thought the lift from a cliff-side would work. I shattered my wing hitting the ground. It was a hard lesson and an even longer recovery."

"But you did recover."

"A long recovery, which was mostly mental. It also included going back to shape-shifting school," Narsus cautioned. "As well as getting yelled at by three gods."

"Cal, the Grim, and Great-Grandfather Acanthus?" Lune teased.

"It's not funny. This is dangerous. Lune, love. I saw you struggling to breathe. To work your tails for the first time. I...I thought I lost you. I don't want to see that kind of distress again. Learn control and how to breathe when you shift."

"My control's fine."

"In your human body, in the shallows. But not in your shifted form, and not so far down," Narsus stressed.

Lune mulled that over. "Cal always tried to teach me, but I wasn't interested."

"You should be aware you're using different organs, or enhanced organs. Different parts of your brain, or a new piece of your brain that grew with the shift. Learn to read your body. Especially breath control between your lungs and gills. I can't help but remembering you telling me you get dizzy—"

"—Coming back to the surface after being down several hours," Lune finished. "Maybe you should help me practice." He batted his eyes. "Being experienced and all."

Narsus eyed him. "Of course. But no shortcuts," he warned. "Shifting and living in a new form is serious business."

Lune twisted his lips in half amusement, but didn't push his luck with a snappy answer.

The bedroom door flew open. Both men appeared, their luggage in hand. "Cinder's uh, coming with me. He says I'm unstable and need a guardian."

"I'm...uh...ferrying him to Temple Prime," Cinder reported, acting just as agitated as Brightside. "It'll be quicker flying."

Narsus frowned at Cinder's unusual behavior before acknowledging the elf. "Bree, I won't keep you. I know you already wish you had miles under your feet. Stay safe, both of you, and come back soon."

"Not soon," Brightside corrected, voice faint and distracted. "But I will. Goodbye my friend. Goodbye, Lune. I'm glad to have met you. And thank you. Thank...you...so much for this." He gripped his compass in a shaking hand. "Take care of this old bird for me."

"I will," Lune said.

"Goodbye." Brightside nodded, and the duo hurried away from the beach house.

Chapter 24

"WELL..." LUNE REMARKED AS the screen door clacked shut. "Now that we have the place all to ourselves..."

"What did you have in mind?"

Lune lowered eyelids and offered a crooked smile. "I want to see what it looks like. Care to assist?"

"What?" Narsus teased. "I thought you were so set on waffles."

"Waffles can wait, Mister. To the bedroom!"

Without a reply, Narsus carried Lune into their suite. Lowering him to the soft mattress, he ran his hands over Lune's dual tails.

Narsus leaned down and kissed the Compass-rose pattern set into the scales of Lune's butt cheek. "Your birthmark is exactly like mine."

"Time to drop your drawers and share." Lune laughed.

"Soon," Narsus said. "You wanted to look at yourself."

"Truuueee."

"So, in order to see what you want to see, we'll need to do *this?*" Narsus's hands journeyed up to the juncture of Lune's core.

Lune gasped a most affirmative yes.

Narsus lifted his brows and stilled his hands. "Ah. So that remains a sensitive area."

"You...thought different?" Lune gasped out.

Narsus hummed. "As if you didn't."

"Well, push deeper. Whatever you're doing is giving me a boner."

Narsus's attention turned downward. Lune was eager for his touch, the twin tails writhing and coiling.

"Oh, *Oh!*" Lune yelped as he assumed what was his dick emerged. Correction: plural? "Well, um. That's...different."

Tentacles. Four of them. Wide-girthed at the base and tapering down into long, thinner ends. Each limb had suction cups. They moved independently of each other in slow, semi-lethargic twitches.

"Lovely. Hello," Narsus greeted them. "How are you? It's very nice to meet you."

Lune choked out uncontrollable laughs. He put his hands to his face. "You're talking to it?"

"Of course," Narsus defended. "Imagine how you would feel, emerging into the world all new and confused, only to be turned away by negativity?"

"It's um...strange."

"You sound disappointed. Why?"

"I had something like that for lunch the other day," Lune remarked with flat ambiguity.

"Ohh, what a marvelous idea. Let's eat."

Lune giggled and hid his face in the pillow. "I...I can't believe we're going to do this."

Narsus chortled, and Lune felt the bed give as his mate gave him some space. "Why?"

The short distance gave Lune the courage to face him. "Well, I...I...wasn't raised to—"

"Is this the same Lune who spent all the birthday money he socked away, like a little squirrel, to have a night out on the town with a courtesan?"

"That's different," Lune protested from his hiding place now under the pillow. "It was for educational purposes only."

"You were brought up by Calico, Mr. Prim and Proper," Narsus mused, poking at the pillow, then gently pulling it away. "I'm not surprised."

"We will *NOT* be talking about Calico right now." Lune was laughing hysterically again. Tears tracked down the siren's cheeks as he motioned to his members. "This is just so...so weird."

"Not weird," Narsus defended. "It's you."

"A good weird," Lune corrected, then stretched out on the bed. "I think. Yeah, I want to show you something."

"What?"

Dreamy eyed and seductive, Lune propped himself up on an elbow. "Watch what I can do."

One of the tendrils lifted. Then, like a finger, crooked a come-hither motion at him. With Lune laughing through it all.

"That was quite the enjoyable treat." Narsus's husky voice was thick.

Lune's nostrils flared as he took a breath. "There're suckers on the undersides. I don't know if I have that much control over them yet."

"So what you're saying is there may be marks afterward." Narsus wiggled his eyebrows.

"That's what I'm saying."

This time it was Narsus's nostrils that flared. "That's a risk I'm willing to—"

He was cut off by the beach house's front door clicking open. Caught by the wind, it slammed against the wall before it was wrestled close.

"Did you hear that?" Narsus nearly growled.

Lune looked up from his immersed self-study. "Hear wh—"

Beyond, in the living room, slow footsteps strode across the planked floor. As if taking in new surroundings. The steps began anew, coming down the hall before stopping at their bedroom door.

Narsus leapt up and flared his wings as the handle turned.

Chapter 25

THE COCKATRICE FROM TEMPLE Prime stood there.

Lune noted he was still clothed in dull, dark grays. He still wore his metallic helmet, with the visor of curved, lemon-colored glass shielding his face. And yes, the glowing compass was still hanging on his belt.

But why? Why was he here?

Lune knew he shouldn't be staring through that magical glass shield for any prolonged period. But the once cultured way of how the man carried himself at Temple, had cracked. A haggard aura battled with the norm of grace and propriety. The shadow of a beard clung to his jaw, and there were bags under his eyes.

Lune grabbed Narsus's wrist before his mate lunged forward into a confrontation. "He was at Temple Prime," Lune wheezed out. "He's one of us."

Narsus halted his advance. His wings flared out, blocking Lune from view. Lune merely grabbed a handful of green feathers and parted them to peek out.

Narsus snapped his wing to block the view again. "Keep your eyes closed, Husband," came the curt, strangled command. "He is a cocka-trice."

Clandestinely, Lune disobeyed. If this stranger wanted to harm them, the face shield would already be raised.

The cockatrice studied his compass, then bowed his head. He backed out of the room. "My apologies. Again, I have been misdirected. You may call me Tryce. I—will wait for an audience upon the beach. I have questions."

Then the intruder was gone, with only the clack of the screen door to bump them out of their surprise.

· ♥ · ♥ · ♥ · ♥ · ♥ ·

"I know him," Narsus announced into the shocked silence. "I met him once when I was very small—when I lived with the Grim. Long before my compass ever manifested. He hasn't changed at all."

"So he was already an adult when you knew him. Who is he?" Lune asked.

"A distant cousin, I'm pretty sure. Related through my Verdigris bloodline."

"That'd make sense. What're you going to do?"

Narsus shrugged. "Talk to him. Find out why he's here."

"That compass has been leading him all around two islands, all this time," Lune mused. "And both times Brightside and I were in his path. I don't envy the adventure he's been through."

Narsus sighed and rubbed a hand across his face. "I...I hope this isn't another Compass-glitch. Not with you."

Narsus startled when Lune grasped his shoulder. "I don't think so. After all, we did just uncover Bree's."

Narsus jerked in surprise. That important piece of information had slipped his mind, given the immediate circumstances. "You mean—?"

"Well, this Tryce did reject attempts at conversation. Twice. So he knows he and I aren't a match. That leaves only one other person. Brightside."

Narsus gave a little huff of hope. "Please let it be."

Lune reached for his trousers, working to stuff his tails through the pant legs while slowly morphing back to his human-self. He smacked himself in the thigh, trying to hurry up the change. "I'm going with you."

"I'm—not sure that'll be a good idea, Songbird."

"Why?"

"If there's an accident, I at least have some immunity to his gaze, being a poison phoenix, and our races are related." Narsus was up, dressed, and heading outside.

"Still going with you." Lune jumped in front of him, his legs morphing fully back into legs.

Lune tried to lead the way up the beach, but Narsus waved at him to walk behind. With eyes downcast as a safety measure. Lune didn't argue and after a second to mull that over, was in complete agreement.

Tryce loitered several yards away, where the tide lapped against the sand. He'd taken off his shoes and seemed to be entranced with the draw of the ocean, stepping a little further into the wet sand when the water withdrew. Their uninvited guest savored the next rush of the waves against his toes.

Perspiration gathered at Narsus's armpits. Tryce appeared to enjoy the essence of the current.

Lune was of the current, the ocean.

Before Narsus could say anything, Tryce faced him.

"Greetings, son of the Grim. Greetings to your mate. Congratulations to you both."

Narsus was taken aback. Lune and Tryce crossed paths at Temple Prime's Compass office, yet Tryce didn't know Lune's name? It was a clue that Tryce really wasn't here for Lune.

Still, Narsus was cautious. "You remember me."

Tryce nodded. "Your sire praises you often."

Hearing that made him proud. "So, what brings you to visit out in the middle of nowhere?" Narsus got straight to the point. He couldn't take the mystery any longer, and he was glad Lune was letting him handle this.

Tryce lifted his compass, holding it between two fingers. To Narsus's relief, it was no longer glowing. "It's been leading me on a wild chase."

"I see that."

"Which has me inquiring. Any of your Compass-companions recently depart?"

Narsus nodded. "They both just left for Temple Prime."

The disappointment that subtly overtook Tryce's body language had Narsus feeling a little guilty at trying to get rid of him so quickly.

"What are their names? Who's compass was it that glowed?"

"Brightside's," Narsus answered.

"Brightside." The name repeated softly on Tryce's lips. Then he frowned. "Brightside. That was the elf who escorted your mate on the road from Temple. He too, loitered within the walls of the temple."

"Yes," Narsus clarified. "He was my proxy to Lune."

Tryce's frown deepened, his deadly eyes lowered in thought. "I was in close proximity with both Brightside, and Lune. Neither seemed to properly match." He lifted a weary hand to toy with the fit of his helmet. "Blast this chaotic Compass-magic."

"If you hurry, your flight might catch up with them."

"I didn't fly here. I can't." He tapped at the visor shielding his eyes.

"Right," Narsus replied, somewhat embarrassed.

"Might I still get a boat back to Staritti's Island? Tonight?"

Narsus shook his head. "Not at this hour, I'm afraid. You'll have to wait until tomorrow. We do have a spare room, if you'd like to stay. You can get an early start."

Tryce didn't answer. Then, "I should not."

"Please," Narsus insisted. "I *know* how much of a burden that helmet is. You'll have your privacy."

There was a defeated sigh. As if Tryce was holding onto the last thread of both his mental, and physical strength. "You *do* know what this portable prison is like, don't you? Yes, you very much do. I will take you up on your offer. Thank you, son of the Grim. Thank you, too, Lune, for this opportunity to catch my breath. This confusing marathon-chase has taken a toll. I promise to be gone before dawn breaks."

Chapter 26

NARSUS HAD PERSONALLY SETTLED their unplanned guest in for the night. By cooking him a meal. Securing Lune's old room by closing the slider glass wall and tying curtains into place. So Tryce could sleep in peace without a helmet wrenching his neck.

And now the stars were glittering brightly through the big, circular window of the bedroom Narsus shared with his husband. The muted sounds of the lulling surf washing away the day's trial.

When Lune walked in from the bathroom, a mild scowl flattened his mate's mouth. "Are you all right?" Narsus asked, worried. "No pain from your transformations?"

"No, I'm fine. Just stewing a little. Please don't take this poorly. I'm glad we're providing Tryce a safe place for the night. Knowing what you've been through with your own mask... It has me realizing how much of an exhausting responsibility it is to protect those around you—*every second.* But..."

"What?" Narsus sat on the mattress and peeled off his boots. He held out his arms, and Lune slid into them. Narsus reveled in the closeness and intimacy.

"Don't you realize?" Lune motioned at the bed. "We're back where we started."

"What makes you say that?"

Lune patted the sheets, slight frustration in the motion. "There's only one bed. Again."

A sly grin washed over Narsus's face. "That's a problem?"

"Of course it is," Lune argued with mild spice. "Especially since it was *you* who invited Tryce to spend the night."

"I couldn't leave my best friend's Intended out there, alone, to sleep all exposed on the beach." He offered an extra squeeze and a cuddle. Brushing his nose against Lune's cheek. "I also recognize how much stress this throws back on you—how much stress *I've* put you under in the last few days. You're reliving all that same agony, again, through Tryce. It's awful of me to make those decisions for you, and grossly unfair. I *will* make this up to you."

The Brightside-Tryce pairing raced back into Narsus's thoughts. He untangled himself from the hug and slowly started pacing back and forth.

Lune lifted an eyebrow. "What's wrong?"

Narsus ran a hand through his hair. "I don't know. Tryce...doesn't seem to fit with Bree. Ah, now it's your turn to not mistake me. Tryce is highly respected. And liked. I've never heard anything bad about him."

"You're being a very good and protective friend. But you have to let them, and the compasses decide."

"Maybe. Maybe I'm still traumatized by the mismatch with Cinder."

Lune scooted to the edge of the bed. "You're too used to Bree and Cinder's easy camaraderie. I've noticed their subtle, *and* flamboyant flirting. Some of the sexual tension between them. They hardly ever came out of their room."

"They were giving us our space," Narsus clarified.

"Are you sure? They seem very good together. It would be a smart match."

The thought of Brightside and Cinder together strangely made Narsus happy. His friends were very comfortable together. It was obvious, especially at Brightside's cottage. But now there was the mystery of Tryce and Brightside's compasses flashing at the same time.

"A match, possibly, but not a Compass-match. Bree and Cinder live together. Cinder's compass has never activated. Ah!" The idea popped into Narsus's head. "Maybe if I meditate, I can reach Bree via his telepathy and give him a heads up. It'd be a long shot though. He doesn't have much of a telepathic range."

Lune launched himself and plowed Narsus back into the bed. "No you don't. You let Bree and Tryce figure it out."

Lune was right. He had to distract himself from interfering. "Why don't you show me the boat you named after me?"

Lune made a stink face. "The boat I named after *you?*"

Narsus grinned back. "Yeah, after me. Compass-matched, remember?"

Lune flopped onto the mattress. "Sorry. Sachin still has her out on hire. The harbormaster'll send a messenger whenever he breezes back home. I hope it's soon, though. I miss my boat. I want my boat. I miss Sachin, too."

"Well, if I can't see your boat yet, I can still fly us to Temple—"

"Will you stop with that?" Lune rolled on Narsus, then sat on him, pinning his wrists against the mattress. "This is our first night, being able to freely touch. And play. Without clothes between us," Lune complained. "But we're filling our time with talk about your friends. And you invite a stranger who's also a distant relative to stay."

"It was the right thing to do."

Lune pouted. "I *get* that. And I'm glad of it, too. But I wanted us to get to know each other, *in private,* now that we're *actually bonded*. After everything we've been through. We've earned it. I know it's just one more night, but I can't help feeling so incredibly frustrated and guilty over my selfishness."

"We still can play, my songbird."

"Not while the walls are so thin."

Narsus gasped. "I knew it. You just wanted to take advantage of me. To see me naked again while wrecking bookcases and knocking knickknacks to the floor. How would Cal put it? *You...you...lustful rogue!*"

"You're so astute," Lune said dryly, arms crossed.

"Well," Narsus offered in all sincerity. "I do have a wedding present for you, to put you in a better mood. Well, it's not really from me. Although, I have been thinking about getting you something nice. Just not sure what yet. It'll have to be big, though. I meant what I said about making it up to you." Narsus pulled a folded piece of paper out of his pocket. "I found it on the table when you were in the bath."

With eager curiosity, Lune unfolded it. He put a hand over his mouth as he read. "It's...from Cal."

"I know," Narsus reminded.

"He's...he's..."

"Soundproofed our bedroom via long distance magic," Narsus confirmed. "Just like he did with the fireproofing. From where ever the God of Space and Time decided to live out his days with his own chosen mate."

"Oh great gods. Nar, do you know what this means?"

Laughter came before the answer. "I don't know. What?"

Lune grinned and yanked off his night robe. "*Now,* without any further interruptions, or distractions, I *finally* get to see your butt birthmark!"

Arriving in 2026

The Compass-Born Trilogy

Book 2: Compass Of My Always
Book 3: Title being finalized

If you are eager to revisit Narsus and Lune with a more vampiric adventure, rather than a focus upon their Compass-born journey, drop me a line at info@bennubright.com and let me know!

The Verdigris Forge: Narsus's forge

- Primary fire color & body color: shades of (iridescent) greens with or without blue highlights

- Body type: rooster-like

- Eyes: usually shimmering green

- Traits/abilities: Immune to all poisons, toxins, and venoms. If there isn't enough of those substances in their system, they can become ill. They can spit venom.

- Culture/society: Hatchlings and juveniles are never seen outside of the clan. Like most other phoenix clans, they can vocally mimic other people/creatures.

- Clan deity/guardian: the Verdigris Archibennu

- Deity of: poisons, toxins, and venoms

The Breese Forge: Calico's forge

- Primary fire color & body color : shades of white, cream, and alabaster

- Body type: like the secretary bird

- Eyes: usually bright green

- Traits/abilities: Sensitive to psychic energies, with limited space-time capabilities. A kick from their long legs can break boulders. They are the most talented in vocally mimicking other people/creatures.

- Clan deity/guardian: the Breese Archibennu

- Deity of: life, healing

The Cottage Forge: Cinder's forge

- Primary fire color & body color: shades of bright orange with or without yellow/white highlights

- Body type: similar to crows

- Eyes: usually red irises ringed with black, can also be various shades of orange or yellow

- Traits/abilities: They are the most talented in breathing fire. Aerial daredevils. Usually curious, outgoing, and sometimes mischievous. Like most other phoenix clans, they can vocally mimic other people/creatures.

- Clan deity/guardian: the Cottage Archibennu

- Deity of: adventure, travel, friendship, entertainment

About the Artists

Lara Yokoshima is a professional illustrator and comic author from Mexico, and her goal is to become an established creator of Western BL. She is the author of a comic/manga series called "Tango," available in Mexico, Germany and the United States.

Her main style influences are Japanese artists like Wolfina, Tada Yumi and Tetsuya Nomura, but she also finds inspiration from Yoji Shinkawa, Ayami Kojima, Jo Chen, Ilya Kuvshinov and Artgerm.

You can find her work at: https://yokoshima.com.mx/

APHOTICMOTH is a fantasy and horror artist living in the Pacific Northwest of the United States. You can find her/their work at: https://aphoticmoth.carrd.co/

About the Author

GREETINGS, MY FORGES! I'M Bennu Bright. It's been my passion to tell stories that entertain. Larger than life characters and adventures are the foundations of my work.

Born and raised in the San Francisco Bay Area, I spend my days at the keyboard, or attempting to revive an ancient interest for the arts.

Sign up for my newsletter at *www.BennuBright.com* and receive updates on upcoming novels.

Follow me on socials at *https://linktr.ee/bennubright* or use the handy QR code below.